NOT OVER YOU

A SONS OF CAPE COD NOVEL

JODI PAYNE

JODI PAYNE

Not Over You
Copyright © 2021 by Jodi Payne

Edited by Flat Earth Editing
https://www.flatearthediting.com/

Cover illustration by Designs by Morningstar
https://morningstarashley.com/
Cover content is for illustrative purposes only and any person depicted on
the cover is a model.

ISBN: 978-1-951011-58-1

Electronic edition published by Tygerseye Publishing, LLC, September,
2021
Printed in the USA

For my grandparents, Gammy and Grandy, who taught me about family and the importance of tradition. For my friends and family who live or summer on the Cape, and all the amazing memories we've shared.

East Falmouth, and especially Davisville, will always be "The Real Cape Cod" to me. The next round of stuffies and Portuguese sweetbread is on me.

1

"Ladies and gentlemen. Welcome to Boston's Logan Airport. On behalf of your handsome pilots and the charming and witty flight crew, I'd like to thank you folks for flying with us today. The next time you have the urge to go blasting through the skies in a pressurized metal tube, we hope you'll think of us. Remember to take all of your belongings, but if you do decide to leave something behind, just make sure it's something we'd like to have. Enjoy your day."

There was a round of laughter, muted in that weird way everything was while your ears were still adjusting after landing. Scott turned off Airplane Mode on his phone, so it would update from California time to Eastern, and checked his texts. He didn't expect any, but he did have a couple from his sister.

Have a safe flight!
Can't wait to see you, it's been so long.
Have you landed yet?

He looked up from his phone to find the aisle still full and moving slowly. Everyone was always in a hurry to get off an airplane, so there was nowhere for him to go yet. He was too damn tall to stand up and wait the way some people did, stooping slightly under the overhead luggage compartment, so he sat there in his window seat and waited for the plane to clear out enough for him to get up.

It wasn't like he was in a hurry. He didn't have any plans, didn't have anywhere to be. He was just...headed home.

Just landed, he texted back.

Yay! See you soon!

Well, at least Kate would be glad to see him. And Ma. Ma would be too, in her stoic New England way. He told himself that after an awkward moment where they'd all acknowledge that he hadn't been home to visit his family on Cape Cod in years, things would relax and be more normal. Whatever normal was.

He'd hide behind Kate if he had to.

By the time he'd visited the men's room, grabbed a very necessary cup of coffee, and found the baggage carousel, the luggage was coming up. He didn't have to wait too long; his black suitcase arrived on the conveyor belt and right into his hands as if it had seen him first.

He got a little turned around trying to find the rental cars, but eventually he and his coffee were in the driver's seat of a shiny black SUV, and he was on his way.

The drive out of Boston wasn't so bad, even with it being rush hour, but it took him almost two hours to finally roll over the Sagamore Bridge. He knew the route well, but he'd made one slight miscalculation in his planning: two hours in traffic was a long time to be alone with your thoughts. He played with the radio and figured out how to Bluetooth his phone to the car so he could dig up a playlist. He sang along, drummed his fingers on the steering wheel, and marveled at the vacationers with their bike racks and box carriers, paddleboards, kayaks, and coolers. Vehicles so packed to the gills you couldn't see out the rear window. So many people trying to make the most of this last week of a lazy summer before schools started up again and the reality of fall set in.

His had never been one of those families. Scott was a townie, born and raised in East Falmouth, graduate of Falmouth High.

Go Clippers.

He'd been one of the local kids that watched those cars full of tourists come and go every weekend all summer long, hoping one of them would bring him a friend, a summer fling, or even just someone different and interesting to hang out on the beach with. He'd made new friends every summer and said good-bye to them every September.

His coffee ran out long before he crossed the bridge, but he made it onto the Cape and hit the drive-through at McDonald's. There was a long line, but he got in it. He was all in now, right?

Headed home for good.

S cott.
  Scott Borden.
  Well...shit.

"Yeah. Kate was telling me he's expected for their family reunion this weekend."

"Well, that's—I'm sure she'll be happy to see him." Jarlath cringed inside and hid behind the case of lemons Nadine had just handed him off the bed of his truck. He'd assumed Scott would miss the reunion just like every other family event his former friend had blown off since he'd left town. "Ma will be glad, too. It's been a while."

"Yeah, Kate said his mom is excited to have him back home. Five years, she said."

"No, shit. Really?" Jarlath had given up hope when Scott didn't make it home the second Christmas in a row. He should have let it go a lot sooner, but Scott wasn't easy to forget. He couldn't believe it had been five years already.

That little voice in his head called him a liar.

Fine.

Okay, so that was a lie. He knew how many years it had been; it was the months and days he'd stopped counting.

Roughly eleven months ago.

Nadine handed him a case of limes. "Kate said he made a ton of money out in California, huh?"

"I guess. Good for him." Jarlath sat the limes on top of the lemons on his hand truck. He didn't really know how he felt about this news yet; it was the first he'd heard that Scott would be home. He was conflicted, for sure. It would be awkward, and mostly he hated the idea. He just wished Scott would stay away because—and it was ridiculous after all this time, he knew—but a big part of him was still hurt and angry.

Part of him wanted to see that smile again, though, and that was what was causing the weird, fluttery, nervous feeling in his gut.

He missed that smile.

"So, you're over him, I guess, huh?"

Ouch. "Over him? We never dated, Nadine."

"No, I know. But everyone knew you guys were...*you know*."

He snorted. "Our options were limited." They hadn't really been fucking. It was just a lot of fooling around, getting off, and trading blowjobs.

Though a few times he'd let Scott...*you know*.

Just a handful of times. But it had been good. He and Scott hadn't officially dated, but they hadn't been just friends either.

"I'm sure he'll be here at the pub with everyone on Monday."

I hope not. He shrugged. "Who knows if Scott will still be in town? The reunion is Saturday, right?" Jarlath knew damn well when the reunion was. He wasn't blood family, but he'd been invited and was expected to be there. Scott's parents were like his own, after all. Amy had been like a mother to him since high school—even more so, lately—and he'd been helping out with Ned after the stroke. They'd been Ma and Dad to him forever.

"Yeah. Saturday. Like, tomorrow?"

"Right. Tomorrow."

Fuck. He was definitely not ready to see Scott tomorrow.

He rolled the hand truck through the back door and straight into the walk-in. This was Labor Day weekend and the pub he owned would be crazy busy, especially after the parade on Monday. Every summer weekend was busy, but the weeks between the Falmouth Road Race in mid-August and Labor Day weekend could be pretty damn insane. It was the final hoorah for the tourist season. Once the vacationers cleared out, the quieter off-season would begin to set in.

O'Connolly's was the name his father had given the pub, and Jarlath didn't plan on changing it. It was right on the parade route, and his little pub was a pre- and post-parade tradition, packed during the festivities and a line out the door and down the block afterward. It was always a banner day.

"You're going, aren't you?"

"Going?"

"To the reunion? Ezra said we were holding down the fort on Saturday." Nadine was more than capable of managing the floor while Ezra covered the bar. It was all hands on deck all weekend, so they'd have plenty of staff.

"Yeah. I'm going. Ma insisted."

"Of course she did!" Nadine snorted and shook her head. "Don't you worry, we'll be fine."

"I know you will." That wasn't lip service. He'd learned

from his dad that the best way to run a business was never to be the only one that could be depended on to work it. He worked when he could, or when he was needed on a crazy night, and sure, paying two managers bit into his bottom line some, but Nadine and Ezra were good at their jobs and he liked it that way.

But...if going to the reunion meant running into Scott, maybe he shouldn't go. Except Ma would be upset, and he wasn't going to ruin this for her. He'd suck it up and go, say hi to Scott, and steer clear the rest of the night. He'd promised to pick Ned up from the home, because he had a truck. And neither Ma nor Kate could lift Dad anyway.

Though if Scott actually made it home, maybe Ma would ask him to do it instead.

He unloaded and went back with the hand truck to find Nadine had loaded another one up already. Cherries, olives, a couple of cases of juices, a box of little American flag stirrers. "I got that."

Nadine snorted at him. "There's a case of oranges and some paper goods and we're done." She rocked the hand truck onto its wheels and rolled it right past him.

Okay, then.

He grinned and hopped onto the truck bed to grab the remaining boxes. He had some calls to make and orders to place. Work was busy. He didn't have time to worry about Scott Borden.

Much.

Scott parked the flashy rental SUV in the driveway, next to Ma's sensible sedan, and peered at the house through the windshield, stunned by how little had changed. The bushes were bushier, the trees a bit taller, and the house had been painted, but Ma hadn't changed the color. It was still the same slate blue that it had been his whole life, with black shutters and a white garage door. He didn't know why he expected it to be different—maybe because he knew he'd missed so many things being gone so long.

He shut off the car and grabbed his suitcase, rolling it up the packed shells and sand front walk—something else that hadn't changed—and rang the doorbell.

It took a minute, but once Ma got to the door, it opened quickly and her smile was warm and broad. "Scotty!" She threw her arms wide and he went right into them, hugging her tight.

"Hey, Ma."

"Oh, Scotty. I'm so glad you got here safely. Come in, come in. Let me look at you."

He didn't think he'd changed much. He was still the

same tall guy he was when he moved away, not much of the football player left in his shoulders maybe, but he did still run. He set his suitcase aside and ran his fingers through his blond hair, straightening himself up for Ma's inspection.

"My handsome boy. I have missed you so much."

"I missed you too, Ma. I know it probably doesn't seem like it, but—"

Ma held her hand up. "It doesn't matter, Scotty. It's not important. I'm just so glad you're here now."

He nodded and hugged Ma again.

"Are you hungry? I've got some macaroni in the refrigerator you could warm up."

"That sounds great, Ma. Is it okay if I take a quick shower first?"

"Of course. I made your room up for you."

"Thanks, Ma. I'll take my stuff up and shower quickly, and then we can have something to eat and talk. Sound good?"

Ma smiled. "That sounds wonderful. Go on ahead."

"Thanks, Ma." He kissed her cheek, grabbed his suitcase, and went up the staircase, which felt even narrower than it used to, to his room, which was essentially the same room he'd grown up in.

He sat on his bed with a sigh. It was weird not having Dad there, though his reception probably wouldn't have been as warm. He wondered if Dad would be able to come to the reunion. He assumed not, but he'd have to ask Ma to be sure.

He looked around the room, remembering everything: his high school football trophies, several of them; his one elementary school spelling bee ribbon; his Star Wars action figures; books and journals; a shelf of CDs.

Pictures of him in his football uniform. His graduation

party. A picture of him and—and Jarlath. There were a bunch of those. Some in high school and some after, when he was tending bar at O'Connolly's.

Jar had been so handsome. He doubted that had changed either.

In his heart, he'd known Ma would forgive him for staying away so long. He figured everyone would eventually, except maybe Jar. And that was going to be tough because he wanted Jar's forgiveness most of all.

Jesus, he felt like a fuckup. He'd followed his dream job out to California, the startup took off like a rocket, then crashed and burned like one too. And now what? He didn't have much money, he didn't have a job, and he didn't have any idea what was next.

He'd stay for a while and see how it worked out, but if Jarlath didn't—well, he had a feeling this wouldn't be the right place for him anymore.

Okay. Enough stumbling down memory lane. He had a hot shower and a big bowl of Ma's mac and cheese calling his name.

Everything else—even Jarlath—could wait.

"Can you grab me a bottle of Bushmills, Boss?"

"Really? You're out?" Jarlath looked up from his laptop.

"Only of the one I need." Ezra shot him a toothy grin as the lanky bartender leaned into his office, one hand on the doorknob and the other braced in the jamb.

Jarlath pushed back from his desk. "That's how it goes, right? Which one?"

"Sixteen. Got a suit at the bar looking for the good stuff."

Bushmills 16 was pretty good stuff. The sixteen-year-old single malt scotch sold for eight dollars a shot even at his little neighborhood Irish pub. The twenty-one-year was even better, but Jarlath didn't stock that for patrons. The only bottle he had was the one he kept in a desk drawer for himself. He only had a couple of regulars that asked for it specifically, and once in a while he'd serve it up from his desk, but he just didn't sell enough of anything that high-end to make it worth stocking.

He got up and unlocked a storage cabinet by the door. "A

suit, huh?" He chuckled. "It's Friday night. Tell him to relax and live a little."

"I haven't seen him before. Probably in town on business." Ezra waggled his eyebrows suggestively. "All alone and handsome."

He handed Ezra the bottle of 16. "That's a winning combination."

"You should come say hello. Offer to give him a tour."

"Yeah, yeah." He rolled his eyes. "Back to work and quit trying to play matchmaker."

Ezra laughed. "You're no fun."

"Watch him stiff you on the tip."

"You said stiff."

"Get out of here." Jarlath gave Ezra a playful shove and closed his office door again. He was only half joking. It seemed like the tourists who looked like they had money were often the first to be stingy with a tip.

He sat back down at his desk and finished the food order he'd been working on when Ezra had interrupted him. He'd be getting a big delivery early tomorrow morning, so he was going to have to come into work for a while before picking up Ned and going to the reunion. He needed to stock up for the crowds this weekend.

He finished his orders and submitted them. In a couple of weeks, he'd be ordering the more traditional Irish fare the locals preferred in the off-season, but for now there would still be plenty of demand for stuffed quahogs and steamed little necks, chowder and crab cakes, flatbread pizzas and lobster mac and cheese.

Or *chowdah* and *lobstah* as his dad would have said. Jarlath didn't really have the pronounced salty Cape Cod accent. Most of his friends didn't either. Maybe all the summer visitors from New York made the local accent less of a thing when they were growing up? Or maybe the teasing about *pahking the cah in Havahd Yahd* had finally just gotten to them. Whatever it was, people seemed to be able to tell he was from the Cape, and maybe he did stretch his *r's* some, but he thought it was more about what he said than how he said it.

He closed his laptop and considered pouring himself a taste from that bottle in his drawer, but decided that because Ezra was closing, he'd save it for home. It was damn near ten o'clock, and he'd been at the pub since eight in the morning, so he needed to get some sleep. It was going to be a long-ass weekend of work with a bunch of late nights in a row, even with a time-out for the Borden family shindig, and he was going to need all the patience he could muster.

Jarlath grabbed his hoodie and pulled it on as he made his way out to the bar to touch base with Ezra about his schedule for tomorrow. Secretly, he was kind of hoping to get a glimpse of the handsome suit sitting at the bar too, maybe see something he could fantasize about later.

He could hear the conversation and laughter of the decent-sized crowd before he got there. George Thorogood was on the jukebox, and that made the little hairs stand up on the back of his neck. God, he *hated* that song. Every time he heard that song it would make him think of—

Make him...

Oh, for fuck's sake. Tonight?

"Headed home, Boss?" Ezra had never met Scott, had he?

His stomach twisted, and everything started to move in slow motion as Jarlath approached the bar. The fucking Thorogood song warped painfully, and Ezra's voice dropped into a deep slur like in the movies.

A pair of bright-blue eyes he hadn't seen in five years locked on to his.

Blue like the summer sky. Blue like he hadn't seen since Scott left town. And fuck if he didn't fall for Scott all over again right there.

Goddamn it.

"You okay, Boss?"

Oh, fuck me. It didn't matter that he'd known he would run into Scott eventually. It was still like seeing a ghost. A hot fucking ghost.

Scott's smile hadn't changed; it was just as confident and cocky as ever, with that little sarcastic lift tugging at one corner.

No. He told himself stubbornly. *Nope.* This wasn't happening. Jarlath rubbed at his chest as if that might stop his heart from pounding, and the room abruptly returned to normal.

Jesus Christ, look at him. Scott Fucking-Blue-Eyed Borden in a sharply tailored suit with the same perfect hair and that goddamn knowing smile. Back at the pub. His pub. *Shit.*

"Hey, Jar."

He wished he'd had that shot of scotch in his office after all. "Scott. This is...a surprise." Okay, it wasn't really a surprise.

"Family thing. I'm sure you've heard." Scott's smile changed slightly, growing less sarcastic and more sentimental. It was real; Jarlath could see it in his ex's eyes. "I was hoping I'd run into you. Do you have time for a drink with me?"

No. He needed the drink, just not with Scott. But, just like before, just like always, "no" wasn't what came out of this mouth. "Sure."

Ezra topped off Scott's drink, put an empty glass on the

bar, and poured a couple of fingers of whiskey in it for Jarlath.

"Thanks." He picked up the glass gratefully and took a sip, half hoping the initial burn would wake him from this nightmare. No such luck. "Ezra, this is Scott Borden. Scott, this is Ezra Macintyre. I hired him after you quit."

"Gave notice."

Jarlath arched one eyebrow. "Four days isn't notice."

"Things move fast in my industry, Jar. I told you. I didn't have two weeks."

Jesus Christ. You haven't changed one bit. What the hell was Scott's "industry" anyway? He'd never been sure. Tech-blah, blah-Silicon Valley, blah-blah. "Isn't this where we left off?"

"Almost. I couldn't afford good whiskey back then." Scott winked at him and took a sip.

He raised an eyebrow. *Asshole.* "Glad it worked out so well for you." *Now get out of my pub.*

"It's nice to meet you." Ezra set the bottle down on the bar between them and disappeared into the stockroom.

Fuck. This would be fun to explain to Ezra tomorrow. "I do know about the reunion, but I didn't think you'd show."

"I decided to take a vacation." Scott rested a forearm on the bar, and Jarlath couldn't help but notice the pair of platinum-and-onyx cufflinks that stood out against Scott's crisp, white shirt cuff. "I missed the place."

Oh, bullshit. Jarlath shrugged, straightened the hoodie on his shoulders, and took another sip of his drink. Something was up. You didn't come back to a little nowhere tourist town on vacation after five years in an "industry."

Scott must have sensed his disbelief. "Actually, Ma basically threatened to disown me if I didn't show. But sweetly. You know how she is."

Now *that* he could believe. Amy Borden wasn't a woman

to take no for an answer. She was a force to be reckoned with, and Jarlath had always loved her. "Sounds like her."

But that meant Scott might be in town for more than a day or two.

Dammit.

"You know, I'll be looking to get out of the house this weekend if you need some help around here."

"You might wrinkle that expensive suit." There was no way he was asking Scott for help.

"Funny." Scott rolled his eyes and finished off his drink. "You'd be doing me a favor." They stared at each other for a long moment, and he wondered if Scott was doing exactly what he was doing—trying to figure out what to say. And how much. "You want to take a walk on the beach?"

God, yes. But, no. Really no. He had to say no. "Thanks. I was just heading home."

Scott watched him, head tilting slightly. "Okay...can I offer you a ride?"

"No, I have my truck. Thanks." Though in fairness, he'd been all about his bicycle the last time Scott saw him, so the offer wasn't as out of place as it seemed.

Scott pulled out his wallet, dropped cash on the bar, and set a business card on top of it. "My cell is there."

He didn't look at it, and he wasn't going to pick it up. Not while Scott was watching, at least. "Give my best to your mom."

"Sure...night." Scott sighed and slid off the barstool, only glancing back at him once before leaving.

Good fucking God.

Scott was five years hotter than he'd been when he left town.

"Excuse me?"

A wave down the bar caught his eye and he snapped out

of it. "Hey, sorry. You caught me daydreaming." He pulled Scott's cash off the bar and dropped it into the tip jar, but he kept the business card. "What can I get you?"

He spent the next few minutes covering for Ezra and not minding one bit. It was a welcome distraction and kept his mind off the business card burning a hole in his pocket. An hour and not one single question about Scott later, Ezra elbowed him. "Am I still closing?"

Ezra was paid hourly and needed the cash. Jarlath understood what he was asking. "Yeah. Sorry. I was just headed out."

"You okay?"

He nodded. "Just don't quit on me with four days' notice."

"Gotcha." Ezra laughed. "Have a good night, Boss."

"You too."

Ezra had been with the bar since Scott left and was a damn good bartender. So reliable that Jarlath promoted him to assistant manager two years ago, then gave the guy a raise when he got married right after the new year. They were coworkers, and they were friends at this point too.

But there were some things he didn't tell anyone, even his friends.

Sure, he was pissed about Scott's lack of notice, but that had been five years ago and even he couldn't hold a grudge that long. What he was feeling now had nothing to do with a bartender taking off without warning. This was something else. Something he didn't expect to be feeling and he didn't want to name it just yet. But he was feeling a lot of it right now.

A lot.

A lot of things he'd thought were in the rearview mirror until those eyes showed up at the pub again.

He sighed and pulled his hoodie back on. *That ship sailed years ago*, he reminded himself sternly. Scott had made his choice clear by not coming home at all, not even keeping in touch. It was better for everyone if they believed he was still upset about Scott bailing on the job.

Jarlath had already closed up his office, so he headed straight for the back door and got into his truck. He'd had it for years, and it was still in great shape despite that scrape along his front passenger-side hubcap. He'd accidentally hit something one winter when Grand Ave along Falmouth Heights Beach washed over with a storm. Probably a curb, but he'd never been sure what it was. That was a storm he wouldn't forget, though. They hadn't had a hurricane hit like that in a long while.

He made his way home, past Acapesket and out Menauhant Road to Davisville. He loved driving over the bridge at Green Pond Harbor and seeing all the sailboats bobbing on their moorings in the moonlight. His family owned a mooring there that he'd used for his own sailboat forever, and like always, he gave her a nod as he drove by.

Jarlath lived just off Menauhant Road, right on Bournes Pond. If you weren't from the area, or maybe a descendant of the Algonquian tribe—*Were there any of those left?*—you'd have no idea how to pronounce half the roads in the area. It was one of a handful of things that marked you as a local and not a tourist.

Meh-nought. Born. A-ca-pes-ket.

Even Scott in his fancy suit would get them right.

Dammit.

Distracting himself from his thoughts of Scott was the reason he'd let his mind wander off on a tangent to begin with. He should have known better.

He parked in the sandy driveway and walked straight

through the house to the back porch, dumping his keys on the hall table and grabbing a beer from the fridge on the way. It was a little chilly at this hour to be hanging out in a rocker maybe, but he wanted a little bracing. He had things to sort out. He needed to clear his head before he saw Scott again at the reunion tomorrow.

He needed a distraction. Maybe he needed a dog.

5

S aturday morning was busy. Despite the jet lag and slight hangover from the night before, Scott had hauled his ass out of bed at eight to drop off his rental car downtown, and then help Ma with the last-minute reunion preparations.

"Scotty, have you finished your coffee?" Ma draped an arm over his shoulders and kissed the top of his head. "Would you mind putting the beer out?"

"Yes. Sure, no problem."

"Thank you, son. Kate will be here soon to help, but neither of us can really carry—"

"No, of course. I got it, Ma." He took the last sip of coffee from his mug.

"There are a couple of coolers in the garage, and you'll see the cases along the wall that Jarlath delivered yesterday."

Jarlath.

"I'll find it." He had lived here once. He got up and kissed Ma's cheek, then put his coffee mug in the dishwasher.

"It's good to have you home, Scotty. I do wish you hadn't stayed away so long, but I am glad you're here now."

"Thanks, Ma." He knew there was probably more he should say, but nothing he wanted to get into on the morning of a huge family party, so he left it at that, gave her a nod, and headed for the garage.

Honestly, he wasn't sure how glad he was to be here. He'd felt a little more hopeful when Kate told him that Jarlath was single, but the reception he'd gotten at the pub the night before had been chilly, to say the least. He'd hoped to talk, or even argue...something. Get a chance to say his piece. Explain himself. Something. But instead, he'd ended up at a bar in Teaticket, drinking alone.

He was such an idiot. He should have known that getting back into Jar's good graces would take more than dressing up and flashing his trademark smile. O'Connolly's and everything about it was practically home for Jarlath. Jar had grown up sweeping floors and working in the stockroom when his father owned it, and it surely meant just as much to Jar now as the actual roof over his head.

And Scott really had quit with four days' notice. He wasn't exactly ashamed of himself, but he could understand why Jarlath hadn't accepted his offer to help.

He moved the coolers first, taking them out to the rented folding table that had been set up as a self-service bar. Ma had a tent too, and tables and chairs. She said they were expecting sixty people. Aunts and uncles, spouses and families, a cousin or six. He'd been surprised by the numbers. He didn't even know there were still sixty people in the family.

He started moving the beer, case by case. *The beer Jarlath had dropped off.* Well, of course he had. Scott wasn't surprised; Jarlath and his mother had been close before he left town. Jarlath had always been one of those friends that could show up for dinner unannounced, and Ma would just find him a chair. It made sense that Jar was still helpful, still present as Ma got older, especially with Dad in a home now.

Shit. He was going to have to go see Dad soon, he knew. Ma told him that Dad wasn't...himself, wasn't "quite all there." It was the first Scott had heard that he'd been having enough trouble that Ma had been unable to care for him on her own anymore, and she wasn't forthcoming with too many details about that. He needed to talk to Kate and find out what he didn't know.

"Scotty!"

Scott looked up from the case of beer he'd just set down and smiled at Kate, who'd sneaked into the backyard through the side gate. The beach gate, they'd always called it. It didn't lead to the beach, but it was the gate you came through when you came home so you didn't get sand in the house.

"Hey, sis."

"I'm so glad you're here." Kate dumped her purse on the table and threw her arms around him. He laughed as he hugged her; he couldn't help it. Kate was the most honest person he'd ever known, and she was honestly glad to see him right now. "I'm so happy you're home."

"Thanks, it's good to see you too. You look amazing."

"Oh, stop." She smiled, though, appreciating his compliment. "Jim is getting the ice, he has tons of it in his truck. And I can't wait for you to meet the boys."

His nephews had been born after he'd left for the west coast. Aiden was four now, and Noah was two. He had plenty of pictures, but it was true, he didn't know either of them.

Damn. The regrets were starting to stack up.

"I can't wait. I'm not too bad with kids, you know."

"Good, you can babysit sometime so Jim and I can get out of the house." Kate winked at him.

"Where do you want it, honey? Oh, hey there, Scott. Long time no see." Jim rolled a wagon full of ice over to him and shook his hand.

"Good to see you again, Jim." Jim looked older but he was still handsome, and Kate still looked so proud of him. "I'm just getting that figured out. Where do you think we should put the coolers?"

"Um. Well?" Jim looked at the table. "How about we put a cooler at either end of the table, and put the wine and glasses on the table. Then people can get to the table to pour."

"Works for me." Scott picked up one cooler and Jim grabbed the other, and they got to work filling them with ice and beer. "How are things? You been good?"

Jim nodded. "The hardware store is solid, busy. We expanded it last year, doubled the size of the place and added some seasonal stuff."

"Oh, good for you."

Jim nodded. "Kate's been good. She misses you."

"Mm. Yeah, I'm not the best at keeping in touch."

"How long are you in town?"

"I don't really know. I'm not needed out in California, so I'm figuring out what's next for me." He knew what he wanted, but he wasn't at all sure he'd get it.

"Oh, yeah? Well, I hope you stick around a while. I know Kate would like that, Ma too."

He sighed. "I know."

Jim looked up from the case of beer he'd just opened. "Look, man. I'm not giving you shit here, I just know folks are glad you're back, that's all. I'm one of them."

He looked at Jim for a long moment, then smiled. "Thanks, Jim. You're a good guy, I see that hasn't changed."

"I still like to fish. That hasn't changed either, if you're interested one morning this week?"

He tried to relax and just take the invitation for what it was. "That sounds great. Yes. Let's do it."

Jim looked pleased. "Is there more beer?"

"Oh, yeah. Jarlath brought a ton. You think we should bring more out?"

"We could stock some under the table for easy refills."

"We could. I'll show you, come on." So, Jim was still cool. He relaxed, feeling a little better for having found someone that seemed to get it. Someone that didn't look at him as if he were a disappointment.

They spent another hour moving beer and wine and setting up tables and chairs. Jim talked about his kids and his new boat, and Scott found he was happy just to listen and keep busy.

"Look at this! You boys do good work." Ma went to Jim and kissed his cheek, then came over to him and did the same. "I'm sure Jim is happy to have another man around to help him out."

He rolled his eyes. "Subtle, Ma."

"What?" Ma looked at him. "Oh, Scotty."

"I'm with Scott." Jim gave her a teasing grin. "You're implying that I couldn't have handled this on my own?"

Ma looked between them. "Oh. The pair of you. Honestly." She set a stack of tablecloths in Jim's arms. "Those go on the round tables. Thank you."

Scott laughed and took a few off Jim's hands.

"Ma," Kate called. "Jarlath is out front with Dad."

He frowned, eyebrows furrowed. "Jar?"

"Oh, I asked Jarlath to pick him up for me. We can't have

a family party without your father." Ma headed for the house.

"Why did you ask Jarlath?"

"It was before I knew you were coming home for sure. I needed to make a plan and give someone permission to take him away from the...to bring him home. It wasn't personal, son." Ma disappeared into the house.

"Jarlath is a little bit of a golden boy," Jim said, sounding amused. "I married in and gave her grandsons, and Jarlath still outranks me."

"Out-*ranks* you?" He sighed. "Of course he does."

"Are you guys still friends?"

He shook his head. "I don't know, I—"

"Well, look who finally came home!" Dad bellowed from a wheelchair as Jarlath rolled him onto the back porch.

"Oh, sounds like he's having a good day." Jim smiled.

Maybe, but Scott had never seen his father looking weak, let alone confined to a wheelchair. His stomach grew tight, and he had to swallow hard to keep the emotions down. "Hey, Dad." He handed the tablecloths to Jim and jumped the two steps up onto the porch, going right in for a hug. Dad lifted one fragile arm and patted his shoulder.

When he stood up, he was looking right into Jarlath's eyes. He remembered them well. They were so dark, it was hard to make out the pupils. He remembered getting lost in those eyes, and he could do it again. Easy. "Jar."

"Scott." Oh, that was chilly.

"Thanks for your help with Dad."

"My pleasure."

"And the beer."

"Oh. Yeah, sure." Jar nodded. Jesus, this was awkward.

Ma pulled over a lawn chair and sat next to Dad. "Jarlath arranged the tent for me too, and the tables and all."

Jar at least looked embarrassed and rubbed his neck. "It wasn't a big deal, Ma. I have a guy..."

"Well. What would you do without him?" Scott was talking to Ma, but looking at Jar.

One of Jar's dark eyebrows shot up as Jar returned his look. "So...I'm going to give you all some family time, and I'll be back for the party in a bit, okay? I need to change and stop by the pub..." Jar started moving toward the door.

"Of course. Thank you, sweetheart." Ma gave Jarlath a little wave and Kate walked him out.

Sweetheart? He really had been gone a long time. "Jar is coming to the reunion?"

"Well, he's family, dear. Of course he is." Ma didn't even blink, just fussed with Dad's shirt.

"He's—" Family? *Jesus.* He was fucked.

6

"Scott? Is that you, Scotty?"

God, a Cape Cod accent that thick could only belong to one man. Uncle Mark, his mother's older brother. "The very same."

"Scotty! Oh, it's damn good to see you."

"Uncle Mark. It's good—*oof*." Uncle Mark took his offered hand and, instead of shaking it, pulled him into a hard hug.

"It's damn good to see you, kiddo."

He tried to get a breath. "Thanks. You said that."

Uncle Mark let him go, smiling broadly. "What's new? Glad you made it to the reunion. You're in town for a few days, I guess? Your mother was hoping you'd be here. Said she had a hell of a time getting you to come home, though."

"Well, I—"

"Have you been up to the Wharf yet? Oh, the renovations there. You know it's a...what do you call it...a banquet hall now?"

"The old Casino Wharf?"

"Weddings and all, and there's a fancy Italian restaurant. God, you wouldn't recognize the place."

Man, he'd spent many a night at the old Wharf's dive bar and pool tables. Weddings? At the Wharf? Wild. "No, I—"

"Well, you won't believe it. And have you seen your cousin Joanie? She's like *that* big pregnant and man, is she grumpy. Wouldn't want to be Danny right now, I'll tell you."

"Hey, Dad! Come get a beer!" Scott's cousin Eddie waved from the bar. "Whoa, Scotty? Is that you? What do you know? Let's catch up in a bit. Dad!"

"That's my cue. Listen. It's good to see you, kid."

He blinked at Uncle Mark. There was never a need to hold up your end of a conversation with him; Uncle Mark would happily hold it up for the both of you. "Good talk, Uncle Mark."

"Take care, kiddo." Uncle Mark socked him in the arm as he left and Scott winced. Jesus, that was going to leave a mark.

He took a breath and exhaled, puffing out his cheeks as he looked around at everyone. Eddie and Joanie were Uncle Mark's kids. Mark had divorced his Aunt Beth just after Joanie was born. Scott didn't know the whole story, but Aunt Beth's name never came up, and she didn't live on the Cape anymore. Uncle Mark was right—Joanie was as big as a fucking whale. God, poor thing. And in the summer, too. She must be due any minute.

Dad might be having issues, but he was surrounded by family, and everyone was laughing and keeping him entertained. Aunt Jess and Uncle Peter and his favorite cousins growing up; James and his wife, Lita; and Ken and his husband, Hap.

His eyes wandered from there to the part of the family

he'd always been fuzzy on. Ma's cousins all had spouses and kids that lived up and down the Cape, but he could never keep them straight.

Moving on, he found Kate and Jim, and—*oh*. They were talking with Jarlath, who looked as if he'd stepped out of one of Scott's fantasies. Jar was wearing an O'Connolly's T-shirt and flip-flops and had one hand tucked into the pocket of a pair of bright-blue board shorts. The easy smile and the way Jar talked and laughed, gesturing with the hand holding his beer, took Scott back years to long nights at the pub and long days on the beach.

They'd been best friends. Life had been good then.

He understood how important the pub was to Jar's family because he'd worked there too, right alongside Jarlath. It was his first high school job, which became the summer job that helped put him through college. After that, he'd been Jarlath's full-time bartender. Leaving for California had been a young man's rash decision on one hand, but on the other, he'd done it in order to take a dream job with a tech startup in Silicon Valley.

He hadn't known when he left how much he'd miss home. How much he'd miss Jar. How could he? They were just friends, they were young, they were just fooling around.

By the time he figured it out, he'd been hip-deep in cash and working twenty-hour days. You didn't just leave in the middle of that kind of success. He couldn't have if he'd wanted to.

Jim started talking, hands flailing and animated, and when Jarlath glanced up, their eyes met. He didn't know what to expect, but Jar didn't immediately look away. They stared at each other for a long moment. Plenty long to know it wasn't an accident. He tried out a smile finally and raised his beer, but Jar dropped his head, shoulders rounding for a second, breaking their stare.

Fuck. He'd blown that moment with a smile? What the hell was wrong with him?

He went and got another beer.

Eventually, Jim dragged him to the grill and they cooked up dozens of burgers and grilled bay scallops and corn for the masses. There were baked beans, regular and German potato salad, buckets of chips, and Uncle Mark brought stuffies and littlenecks from the harbor fish market.

Stuffed quahogs, or "stuffies" as the locals called them, were always part of a Cape Cod summer party. They were large clams filled with a stuffing made of clam meat, stale bread, bell peppers, and seasonings. His father loved stuffies, particularly the spicy ones.

Scott could not wait. San Francisco was known for its food, but nothing beat a genuine Cape Cod cookout.

Except maybe a clambake on the beach. Oh, he missed those.

"Jim. Jim, did you see this?" Scott and Jim were just cleaning up the grills when Kate brought her phone over and showed it to Jim. "They're calling it Eric."

"No shit, they named it?" Jim took the phone.

"Named what?" he asked, hoping they weren't referring to someone's baby or something as an "it."

"Hurricane," Kate looked at him seriously. "Next week."

Oh. shit. It was hurricane season, and everyone took that seriously on the Cape.

"Well, they're saying maybe Wednesday night into Thursday." Jim handed Kate's phone back. Scott looked around again. Just about everyone's houses were far enough up from the beach that they wouldn't have to board up except maybe Jar's and—

"Jarlath? Jar, come here." Kate waved and Jar came trotting over.

"What's up?"

"Hurricane Eric."

Everyone looked at Jarlath. Jar's house was on Bournes Pond, and that was somewhat of a risk but the pub... O'Connolly's was in the Heights, right on Grand Ave, which ran all along the beach. It was potentially in the path of every hurricane. All of them. Every single storm that came through.

Including this one.

The good news was, they constantly made improvements to the sea wall there, and Jarlath's father had done everything humanly possible to give the building the best chance of survival. The bad news was, nothing that close to the water was ever hurricane proof.

He watched Jar's jaw clench. "All right. When?"

"Right now, it looks like Wednesday night."

Jar frowned and rubbed his forehead. "I just this morning brought in a huge food order and tons of supplies for Monday."

Scott nodded. Labor Day was big. One of the days he knew Jar would count on to support the pub.

Kate rubbed Jar's back. "People will probably stick around until Tuesday."

"I hope so." Jar pulled out his phone and checked the weather, shaking his head slowly. "Shit. It might be a big one, huh?"

Scott felt the mood in the air change. The party was definitely over.

"I bet the parade will still go on, Jar. You'll be okay on Monday." Ma put an arm over Jar's shoulders. "And we'll all come help you close the place up on Tuesday."

"Oh, yeah. We're there, man," Jim chimed in. "Whatever you need."

Jar's eyes flicked up to Ma's, then scanned everyone else's faces. Everyone's but his. "I'd appreciate that."

They wouldn't be alone in helping. Events like this pulled the locals out of the woodwork, laying sandbags, delivering boards and stowing outdoor furniture. Scott remembered one time when Ma and Kate had made sandwiches all day and delivered brown bags to people who were volunteering their time to help others protect their homes and their storefronts.

That didn't mean it wasn't going to suck. It didn't mean it was all going to be okay either. The hurricane could track farther out and spare them and all the preparation would end up having been unnecessary, or it could hit Falmouth like a bull's-eye and no amount of sandbagging would be enough.

The party had been winding down anyway, and pretty soon there were just a few of them left cleaning up. He spotted Jar trying to lift a cooler of ice water and ran over to help.

"Where are we going with this?"

Jar glanced at him briefly, then looked away and took one handle. "Over the picket fence back there." The yard was lined with a thick tangle of scrubby pines.

"Sounds good." He took the other handle, and together they carried the cooler and dumped it over the fence. They worked quietly together for a while. Jar didn't ask for his help, but he didn't refuse it either. They folded up tables and stacked chairs for the rental company and brought the liquor and beer into the garage.

Jarlath had a look around the yard. "I guess that's it. Thanks for your help."

He nodded. "You're welcome. I could use a beer."

"Well, we just put a case in the—"

"I know!" They both turned their heads and looked at the back door when the shouting started. "Dammit, I can play this game. I've been playing Gin for damn near eighty years!"

"Dad." That was Kate's voice.

"Shit." Jarlath bolted into the house and Scott followed.

"Calm down, Dad. It's just—"

"Do not tell me to calm down, young lady!" Dad's eyes were wide and his expression terrified. "Oh, Sean. Thank God. These people are crazy."

Jarlath didn't miss a beat. "Damn right, Ned. It's time to go."

Scott went to his mother. "Does Dad think Jar is Mr. O'Connolly?" Jar was the spitting image of his late father.

Ma nodded. "Jarlath is so good with him when he gets like this. Oh, thank God for Jar."

"Are you okay, Ma?" He took Ma's trembling hands in his as they watched Jarlath and Jim roll Dad out to Jar's truck. Dad was ranting and his arms were flailing, but they all watched through the window as Jar took Dad's hands and spoke to him seriously. A moment later, Dad was letting them help him into the truck.

Ma sighed hard and sat down. "He was having such a good day."

"He was probably worn out, Ma." Kate came and sat too. "It was great to have him back for a while, wasn't it?"

Ma nodded but didn't say anything. Or maybe couldn't say anything. She looked like she was about to cry.

"How about a hot bath?" Ma nodded again, and Scott offered her his arm to help her up.

"I'm sorry everybody. I'm so sorry."

"No, Ma." He patted Ma's hand as Kate came over. "Don't be sorry, it was a fun party. It was a great day."

Ma stopped and touched his cheek. "I'm so glad to have you home, son. My boy. I love you so much."

"I love you too, Ma."

Ma gave him a watery smile and let Kate lead her toward her bedroom. "Good night."

"Night, Ma."

7

Labor Day arrived without any hint of bad weather, and Jarlath was relieved to see everyone lining up to watch the parade. Kate had been right; it seemed like most people did stay in town for the holiday. He'd bet tomorrow there would be a lot of traffic leaving the Cape, but today it really was business as usual.

He parked his truck and climbed out, breathing a big sigh of relief. Not just because he had food that would have gone to waste if people had left town early, but because Labor Day always brought in money, and he was counting on it to help float the pub in the slower fall and winter. Ezra and Nadine were already there, and a handful of others. By the end of the day almost his entire staff would be on shift, some of them coming straight from being in the parade itself.

They'd set up a roped-in area out in the parking lot for when the party got too big to keep inside. He had his permit in place like every year.

"Hey, Boss. Got a minute? We have a small problem." Ezra stopped him right inside the back door.

He rolled his eyes. Of course. "What is it?"

"Bar fridge is out."

"Which one?"

"The bigger one. It's just dead. We hauled it out and plugged in a blender that worked, so it's not the outlet. The thing is gone."

Jarlath sighed. "Well...fuck."

"That's what I said." Nadine touched his shoulder as she walked by them. "Everything else is looking good, though."

Okay. This wasn't the end of the world. There was a Walmart; he'd go buy a couple of small ones to get them through the day and order a new one on Tuesday. "Okay. I'm on it. You all get back to setting up. We have to open in an hour."

"Right. Don't sweat it, Boss, we got this." Ezra turned and headed for the bar, and Jarlath took a breath. He totally trusted Ezra; he just needed to get this taken care of. He turned right around and went to his truck. If he could pick up two little ones, not the cube ones but the taller ones, he'd be golden. One could fit in the space the bigger one took up, and the other could tuck in next to the register. It'd be a little in the way, but not awful.

It would have been a good plan if it had worked out, but it hadn't. Walmart didn't have a single mini fridge. He noted on his way out that they didn't have a lot of anything else either—they'd probably been raided when people heard there was a hurricane coming.

Once he got back in his truck, he made some calls and managed to get a plan B set up, which turned out to be a better plan than his plan A. His buddy Taggart had the exact model of bar fridge he needed to replace the one that had broken. It was secondhand, but Taggart said it was in great shape. The trouble was he had to get to Hyannis, and that was a forty-minute drive without holiday traffic. With the holiday it could be an hour, and he didn't have that kind of time.

He did have family, though. He dialed Ma.

"Jarlath? What's the matter, sweetheart? Aren't you working today?"

"Hey, Ma. Yeah, but we had a fridge go. Is Jim around?"

"No, Jim's in the parade. He always marches with the high school."

Right. Shit. Of course he did, Jim ran an after-school science club. "I forgot. Kate, maybe?"

"No, I'm sorry. She went to help the kids line up and all."

There was a pause while he thought about what he could do. "Okay, Ma. I'll figure it out."

"Scotty's here with me, I can send him over." Ma sounded all too happy to offer up her son.

Jesus. That was all he needed. "No. No thanks, Ma."

"Here, I'll put him on the phone."

"Ma. It's okay, Ma. I got this." He heard the phone rustle as it changed hands, and he knew he was too late. *Dammit.*

"Hey, Jar. I've got nothing but time. What can I do?" Scott's smooth voice actually soothed his nerves even if it was like sandpaper on his heart. "Seriously. I've even got wheels."

Okay. Fine. He'd let Scott do this. He needed the help, and he couldn't wait for Jim.

"I have a friend in Hyannis who has a replacement bar fridge for me." Taggart was one of the good guys. "I'm at the pub, you can take my truck."

"Shit, you lost a fridge? Today of all days? All right, I'll be right there. Sit tight."

"Thanks," he managed to say before the line went dead. "Fuck." The last thing he wanted was to owe Scott a favor.

But Scott knew his way around the Cape and had always been reliable at the pub.

Right up until the day he quit, anyway.

There was a rap at his office door, and Nadine stuck her head in. "We're open."

He nodded at Nadine and stood up. "All right. Let's do this."

———

THE DRIVE WAS LONG, but Hyannis wasn't quite as crazy as he thought it would be, and Scott found Taggart's shop without a problem. It was closed, but a black SUV pulled into the parking lot behind him just as he was getting out of Jarlath's truck.

That was either going to be Taggart or the FBI.

"Hey, there. Scott, right?" The word "there" was two, or maybe almost three syllables, and drawn-out like they had all day.

"That's me. I've got Jar's truck."

"Oh, good call. Drive it around back, yeah? I got a dolly. This thing is wicked heavy."

"You got it." He climbed into the truck and parked near the loading doors so they could get to the fridge.

"Tough break losing a fridge on a big day."

"Yeah, but he's lucky to know you."

Taggart nodded and grabbed the dolly. "I'm closed and we're having a cookout today, but Jar's a good buddy, and I just happened to have exactly what he was looking for."

"Very cool of you to leave your party."

"Eh. It's mostly my wife's family, you know. I'll get back before anybody misses me." They wrestled the low, wide fridge onto the dolly. "So, are you the Scott that Jar used to talk about all the time?"

Used to? He blinked at Taggart. "I don't know. Am I?"

"Your, uh...your mother is Amy?"

"Wow, you really do know Jar well, huh?"

"We go back a few years. He started as a good customer, and we ended up having a few beers one night and talking. After my sister drowned, he stepped up and helped out. Did a fundraiser and set up a college fund for her kids. He's a good guy. Real deal, you know."

"Wow." Jarlath still amazed him.

"I thought you were in California?"

"I was. I'm home for...a little while."

"Well, that's cool. I bet Jar's happy to have you helping out." Taggart stopped the dolly by the tailgate and dropped it. "You know how to work the Tommy Gate?"

"Oh. Yeah. Jar showed me." He unfolded the tailgate and moved around to the side of the truck to push the button. "Easy."

They rolled the fridge onto the gate and strapped it down; then Taggart climbed up and Scott lifted it. They had it strapped into the truck in no time.

"Listen, I can't thank you enough." Scott stuck out his hand to shake and Taggart took it, all smiles. "You give Jar my best, and tell him not to worry, we'll settle up after the hurricane blows through. He can call me."

"Will do. Thanks again."

Taggart gave him a wave and he hopped back into the truck.

———

"Hey, Boss."

"Where are you, Benny? Your shift started at noon." Benny was a good bartender. He wasn't always the most on-time employee, but he'd never been an hour late. Jarlath held the phone to one ear and a hand over the other so he could hear.

"Yeah, man. Listen, I'm really sorry but Celia is in labor."

"Labor Day. Funny." Jarlath snorted.

"Not a joke, Boss. She's having the baby. Now."

Jarlath lowered the phone to his side and took a deep breath. The baby wasn't due for two weeks. The plan was to get through Labor Day and this fucking hurricane; then Benny could have a couple of months off in the off-season. It timed out perfectly.

But babies don't always go to plan.

Babies are a cause for celebration! He can't control Mother Nature. The baby is coming. This is Benny, man. Breathe.

He swallowed and put the phone back to his ear.

"Boss? You there?"

"Yeah. Yeah sorry, Benny. Someone asked me a question. Listen, congratulations, man. I hope everything goes great. Text me a picture when you know if it's a boy or a girl, okay?"

"Yeah. I'll do that. I'm really sorry."

"Don't be. This is great news. Good luck with everything. Give my love to Celia."

"Thanks, Boss. You're the best. I'll check in when I know something."

"Talk soon." He hung up the phone. *Fuck. Fucking fuck.* Short a bartender on Labor day.

Fuck.

"Ezra!"

"Boss?"

"Benny's not coming in. His—"

"What? Fuck. What the—"

"Celia's in labor." Jarlath shrugged.

"Oh." Ezra sighed. "Gotcha."

"Yeah." They were both feeling the same way. Happy for Benny, but the timing was going to make today suck just a little.

"Well. We've got this." Ezra shrugged.

"We've totally got this." Like they had a choice.

"Is the fridge—"

"Let me call Scott and see where he is. You okay for a few more minutes?"

Ezra grinned at him. "I live for the weeds."

He gave Ezra a nod and ducked out back to call Scott. As it turned out, Scott was just pulling into the driveway. Thank God something was going right. He waved Scott over to the loading area so they could get the fridge right off the truck, and Scott backed it up as if he knew what he was doing.

Jarlath opened the tailgate and climbed into the bed to loosen the tie-downs.

"Everything okay inside?"

"Getting busy but so far so good. Thanks for doing this."

"Happy to help. Taggart's a good guy. He sends his best."

He nodded. He'd been really lucky to inherit a lot of Dad's vendor contacts, but Taggart was one of the first business relationships he'd built on his own. He was a good guy. Honest, friendly, and obviously willing to step up when Jarlath needed him. That earned his loyalty and, in this case, friendship too.

They rolled the unit off the truck and right through the back door.

"Whoa. Oh, it's here, awesome. Hang on." Nadine cleared a path for them, moving things, picking up floor mats, and holding the door as they wiggled it behind the bar. Jarlath plugged it in and it started right up, so they pushed it into place, exactly where the dead one had been.

"Perfect!" Jarlath let himself grin. "Thanks for your help, Scott."

"You're welcome. Do you—"

"We needed a break, huh? Looks great." Ezra squeezed by them, drinks in hand.

"Damn right." Jarlath sighed. "Okay. Nadine, I'm going to give it an hour, and then can you help me stock it up? Benny's not coming in."

Nadine's eyes went wide. "He's not? Can you manage this with just two of you?"

"Not much choice." He winked at Nadine.

"You're short?"

Oh, shit. He forgot Scott was standing there. He really did appreciate the errand, and maybe he and Scott could find their way to being friendly acquaintances eventually, but no way was he letting Scott behind his bar again. He stood up tall and took a step forward like he was going to walk Scott out. "We're good, thanks."

"Hey, it's been a while, but if you need help, I can totally step in."

"Ezra and I have got it, Scott. Thank you." *And good-bye, please.*

Scott sighed and shook his head. "Suit yourself."

"Hey, Jarlath!" A couple of local guys flagged him down from the end of the bar.

"Coming, guys." He gave Scott a look and made his way down to see what they wanted to drink.

———

SCOTT DUCKED into the office and dropped the keys to Jarlath's truck on the desk. He couldn't help but linger for a moment, remembering Mr. O'Connolly sitting in that same chair, giving him a smile and handing out unsolicited good advice, a paycheck, or a holiday bonus. Jar's father had understood Jarlath in a way that Scott's father refused to understand him. Secretly, he'd been a little jealous, but for his acceptance and for always leaving the door open to talk, Mr. O'Connolly would always be a father figure to him.

Scott sighed and left the office, saw himself out the back door, and decided to walk around to the front and watch the parade. It was tough getting into the parking lot with everyone crowded at the finish line; he wasn't even going to bother trying to get out yet.

The high school band had stopped and was finishing off a song, with several flag twirlers spinning maroon flags with white clipper ships on them.

Go Clippers.

He got himself into the crowd where he could be anonymous and not feel so by himself and cheered with everyone else.

It wasn't long before Jim and Kate marched over the finish line with Jim's gaggle of high school science club members carrying signs. One read "A Moment of Science," another said "Prove it," and a third one read "We've Got Chemistry." It was so perfectly small town, he couldn't help but smile. Jim caught him in the crowd and waved, then pointed to the pub.

He gave Jim a thumbs-up, assuming that meant they were going inside after. He wasn't sure he should, though— Jar had practically thrown him out a minute ago.

Jarlath sure knew how to hold a grudge—not that Scott blamed him.

He wanted another chance, though. He hadn't known that for sure until he'd come home but now that he was here, he couldn't stop thinking about making it up to Jar. He wasn't sure if there would still be a spark, but he wanted to find out.

"Scott!" Kate shouted and waved him over.

He waved back and worked his way through the crowd to her. "This is crazy!" The parade was winding down, though, and he could see the fire trucks that brought up the rear just down Grand Ave.

She nodded. "Not everyone stays at the pub after, but a lot of people do. It's nuts. You want to head in for a beer?"

Did he? "I don't know."

Kate studied him. "How are you going to find out if you don't go in?"

"Find out...?" He gaped at Kate a second, trying to answer that question. He wasn't even sure exactly what she was asking. Jim saved him, hustling both him and Kate inside.

"Okay, let's go."

He let himself be led inside, still unsure how to handle things. He looked around at the busy pub and the crowded bar. Okay. One beer, then he'd find an excuse to go home. Tonight wasn't the night to try to impress Jarlath, not with the pub so busy and so much going on.

"I'll get us the first round." Jim had to raise his voice to be heard.

Kate gave Jim a wave and pulled Scott over to a less crowded corner of the bar. "So what's up with you and Jarlath?"

He raised an eyebrow. "Nothing is up." Like, literally nothing.

"The two of you gave each other a lot of room at the

reunion." The way Kate crossed her arms and tilted her head just so made her look exactly like Ma. "You barely spoke."

"Kate, why are you bringing this up?"

"Because you might have been gone a while, but I know you."

"Yeah, well. Jar's been here the whole time, and he's clearly the favorite son now."

"Oh, Scott—"

"I know, I know. I haven't been here. He's a big help to her, Jar needed Ma too...whatever. He's a good guy, I know. He's the one that stuck around. He's perfect, and I'm the son that went away and never came home."

Kate's eyes narrowed and she stared at him. "Are you jealous?"

"No. I'm—I don't know, Kate. I'm a little humiliated, I guess."

Kate reached out and touched his arm. "How long are you staying?"

"Well, I can't get out before the hurricane, there aren't any flights."

"That's it? After the hurricane?"

He sighed and shook his head. "I think I might stay for a while. The company's finished, Kate. We closed it down a couple of weeks ago." And he was more homesick than he'd realized.

"Oh. Shit, Scotty. I didn't know that. I'm sorry."

"Well, I haven't told anyone so...how would you know?" He'd meant to say something by now—he'd even tried, but there was never a good time. He'd been about to talk to Ma when Jar had called needing help. He shrugged. "So, I have some money put away but no reason to rush back to the West Coast."

"So are you going to try to talk to Jar?"

"Talk to Jar about what? He's busier than a hippie at a tie-die contest."

Scott peered over at the bar, but he couldn't even see Jarlath for all the people gathered there. "They're short a bartender."

"They are?"

Scott shrugged. "Yeah, he said Benny's wife was in labor."

"She is? Oh, I hadn't heard!" Kate clapped her hands together, looking pleased. "I have a baby gift I can give her now."

Jim returned and handed out bottles of beer. "It'll be a good day, the tip jars are already filling up."

Oh. That was good.

"I keep meaning to ask how long you're in town for, Scotty..." Jim looked at him expectantly.

Scott looked from Jim to Kate.

"He's not sure yet," Kate said quickly, and he silently thanked her.

"Ah. Well, we'll do our fishing trip anyway."

"For sure. Yeah." He was actually looking forward to it.

"Have you been past the high school yet?"

"No, not yet." It wasn't even on his list, but he could understand why Jim asked. Jim was proud to be involved over there.

"Oh. You oughtta go see. I'll take you around." Jim started telling him about all the new construction at the high school, the new gym, a new media center, all kinds of things that had gone on since Scott left town. Scott listened while he drained his beer, enjoying the hoppy flavor of his IPA. The music was going but what was usually a little dance floor was filling up fast with people talking, laughing, and drinking.

"I'm empty," Jim said, reaching for his bottle.

"No, no. You got the last one. This one is on me." He took Jim's instead. "Kate?"

"I'm good." She hadn't even finished half of hers.

"I'll be right back." He headed for the bar. He didn't intend to have another, but he wanted to take care of Jim.

When he got to the bar it was three people deep, and Ezra was handing out drafts three at a time. Jarlath was biting his lip and sweating, and Nadine was stocking but looked like she could barely keep up.

He waved at Ezra so he didn't have to deal with Jar. Ezra looked up, eyes a little wild. "This is insane! You need a beer?"

He started to say yes, but then he shook his head and pushed through the crowd, ducked under the hatch, and popped up behind the bar.

"Scott?" Ezra looked at him, startled.

"I used to have your job."

Ezra's grin was wide and happy. "Fuck, yes! Thank you."

"Don't thank me yet. Jar told me no."

Ezra rolled his eyes. "Jar doesn't like it, I'll pay you myself. I'm the fucking manager, right?"

He wasn't doing it for pay, but he slapped Ezra on the shoulder and nodded. "Point me."

Ezra looked around. "Uh...guys in the sparkly top hats want the Hog Island IPA. Pints."

"On it." He went right to work. His fingers remembered how to pull a beer without much thought, and he found most of what he needed to remember came back quickly.

He'd served up at least a dozen beers before Jar finally noticed him.

"Scott? I said we didn't need you." Jar reached for the vodka and mixed up a cocktail.

"Like hell you don't."

"I don't want you back here."

"I know. But Ezra does."

"Ezra—" Jar looked over at Ezra, who was busting his ass at the other end of the bar.

"The manager hired me for this shift. You want me to go? You tell him." He dared Jar to go argue with Ezra, who was pouring two drinks and taking orders at the same time.

Jar narrowed his eyes and stared at Scott hard for a long moment.

Then Jar set the vodka on the shelf and walked away without another word.

He was silently celebrating the victory when Jim and Kate waved at him. "Good for you, Scotty!" Kate shouted.

Jim followed that with, "We'll see you later!" and they both turned to leave.

"Rum and coke, please?" A woman shouted at him.

"Two IPAs." That one was waving cash.

"Hey, new guy! A couple of Coors?"

Oh, boy. Maybe this wasn't a victory he needed on his résumé.

———

"Night, Andy. Night, Darla."

Jesus H. Christmas.

Jarlath followed the last of his customers out and locked the door behind them. Then he looked around, taking in the incredible mess. The pub was a fucking disaster. There were overturned chairs, food and garbage everywhere, glasses on every surface—including the window ledges, the jukebox, and the band platform. Through long-standing tradition, Cape Cod bars closed earlier than bars in most other places, and he usually was shut down by one a.m. Tonight it had been a struggle to get everyone to leave by two. He was exhausted.

He knew better than to let it take hold yet, though. This mess couldn't wait until morning; they needed to clean up and set everything right so they could come in tomorrow—well, later today—and open up at four.

He reminded himself to toss a good bonus at his managers tonight. Even with Scott helping out, they'd all been swamped.

He grabbed a tub and started bussing but couldn't help glancing over at Scott behind the bar as he gathered up glasses and bottles. He was willing to swallow his pride enough to admit that Scott had been a huge help today. There wasn't any denying it. But even so, emotionally, he was swinging on a wild pendulum between deeply angry and deeply grateful, and minute to minute, he honestly wasn't sure exactly what he was supposed to feel.

He didn't know whether to say fuck you or thank you.

Maybe he could say both?

"Thanks for doing that, Boss." Nadine interrupted his train of thought.

"Hm? Oh. Yeah, no problem. Ezra and Scott have the bar covered. I'll get a mop in a minute."

There were three other servers cleaning tables and putting up chairs, and still it seemed like they were hardly making a dent.

"Good day, huh? My pockets are full of tips."

"That's the spirit." Nadine had it right. His register was bursting too. He'd had to empty the cash into the safe a bunch of times. "I'm going to have to get back there and put together tomorrow's deposit."

She nodded. "We got this. Why don't you go ahead? Maybe then you can get out of here about the same time as the rest of us."

He gave her a smile and touched her shoulder. "I appreciate that. Thanks." Jarlath filled up the rest of the tub and set it next to the bar for the guys to throw in the dishwasher and recycling.

Ezra gave him a nod. "Thanks, Boss."

Scott caught his eye and looked as if he wanted to say something, but Jarlath pretended not to notice and headed for his office. He went in and shut the door with a sigh. Nope. He had no intention of dealing with Scott tonight.

The final cash drawer was on his desk, and the first thing he did was pull out two hundred dollars. A hundred each for Ezra and Nadine. He needed to keep his A-team happy.

The next hour flew by as he went over receipts and put the cash together. They'd look at the inventory roster tomorrow; he didn't have the brainpower or the patience and he doubted they'd be very busy with the hurricane coming.

Depending on what the weather said in the morning, they might not open at all.

Fuck, the hurricane.

Hell, the inventory should probably wait anyway, given the weather. There was no way to know what would survive the storm and what wouldn't.

He was going to have to head down cellar in the morning, see what they had on hand, and go out and get supplies. He knew he had sandbags, and Dad had commissioned these huge custom shutters for the front that he would put up. But really? This close to the water, it was just a matter of luck. Could be good or could be bad.

Either way, it was going to be a long fucking week. What he needed right now was some sleep. The storm wasn't supposed to hit until after dark on Wednesday, so he had some daylight to get things done between now and then. He could sleep tonight.

He locked up the deposit in the safe and went to check on his people, whistling when he stepped into the front of the house. "You guys, it looks like my pub again. You did a great job."

"Thanks, Boss. We sent the crew home, Scott and Nadine and I finished up."

And there was Scott, standing right next to Ezra, looking tired and proud of himself. Jarlath remembered that look. He'd usually get a blowjob when Scott would look at him that way.

Don't even go there, idiot.

He waved his hands. "Let's all head out. We have hurricane prep and a pub to run tomorrow."

"What time do you want us here?" Ezra asked, dumping his apron in the laundry bucket with the bar towels.

He shrugged. "I'll be here about ten to see what we have down cellar."

"I'll come do inventory."

He shook his head. "There's no rush on that, I'm not going to restock until after the storm."

"Oh. Right." Ezra sighed and nodded. "Well, I'll be here anyway."

"Me too, Boss." Nadine rubbed his shoulder.

"Jim and I are planning on coming to help board up. Are you doing that tomorrow or Wednesday?"

He didn't turn Scott down; he was going to need as much

help as he could get. "We'll close on Wednesday and board up then. I'd like to try to stay open tomorrow night." People needed a place to hang out before a storm. See friends. Shake off the anxiety.

"All right. I'm out." Nadine turned to go but Jarlath stopped her, pressing her bonus into her hand. She gave him a big smile. "Thanks, Boss. Sleep well."

"Good night." He handed some cash to Ezra too. "Tell Lisa I'm sorry for keeping you away from her and the baby." He knew Ezra needed the money, but Ezra was a devoted dad who missed his family.

"Thanks. Lisa's mom has a generator, so I think we'll all stay there through the storm. Our house will be fine. I've got lots of time to help, don't you worry."

"I'm not worried." That was bullshit, and he figured everyone knew it.

"Uh-huh. See you tomorrow. Thanks for this. Thanks again for jumping in, Scott." Ezra put the cash into his pocket and went out the back.

And that left him there with Scott, who was leaning against the bar, watching him.

Oh. Shit. "I need to pay you."

"No. No, that's cool. It was a favor."

"Okay. Then I guess I owe you one." *Dammit.*

"You didn't throw me out. We can call it even."

"No. No, I couldn't. I guess I...you were a big help." That was hard to admit, but the fact was that he and Ezra had been drowning and he damn well knew it.

"Is that a thank-you?" He knew that smug grin was meant to tease, but it was still exasperating. It set his blood boiling.

"Thank you. Fuck you. God, I wasn't ready to have you

back in here yet." Jarlath turned around and headed for his office.

"Whoa. Okay. I was joking." Scott fell in behind him, following along.

"I'm not."

"Jar, I know you're upset about me quitting. I know we didn't leave things on a good note."

Jesus, Scott was so frustrating. "It's not about how we left things, Scott. It's about how things are now."

"I don't understand. How are they?"

He stared at Scott. "You…abandoned your family. You abandoned your job. You abandoned me. You just…left."

"I had a job to go to, Jar. A good one. Something in my wheelhouse, and a job that I really wanted. I didn't abandon—"

"Oh, bullshit, Scott." Jesus, he was too tired for this argument, and he had no goddamn filter. "You haven't been home in five years. You didn't keep in touch—"

"I called my mother every Sunday." Scott tossed an arm out for emphasis.

"Yeah. I know, because I still go over every Sunday for dinner, just like I did before you left town. I heard all about your phone calls with Ma. About your friends, your job, who you were dating."

"Oh. Shit." Scott looked shocked.

"Yeah. And you called me, hm…let me see if I can remember. Oh, right. Never. Not once. You disappeared off the planet."

"I—"

He stared his ex down. "Not even a goddamn text, Scott. Not even one text."

Scott sighed and leaned against the doorframe, frowning and chewing his lip. For a second, Jarlath felt sorry for him.

Only for a second, though, and he didn't regret letting his feelings out either. They'd been bottled up since Scott left town. He might later, but it was Scott who decided to poke him after a long, hard day and Jarlath already felt raw. He didn't have enough energy left in him for regret right now.

"You're right, I'm sorry," Scott said quietly.

He scanned Scott's face, taking in an expression he knew to be sincere. He'd known Scott very well once, after all.

He wasn't a dick. He wouldn't totally blow off an apology like that, even if he was still angry, but he was so fucking tired. He was about to ask if they could not have this conversation tonight, when Scott turned and left his office.

8

Scott had intended to show up at O'Connolly's Tuesday morning with Ezra and see what he could do to help. As it turned out, he never made it and instead spent his time helping Ma and Jim and a handful of neighbors and family board up and secure outdoor furniture and grills, take down flag poles, and stow anything that wasn't nailed down.

The house—Ma's house—had been through many storms over the years and usually did very well, as long as the shutters were closed and they put sandbags in front of the garage door. He planned to ride out the storm at home with Ma, which Kate and Jim were greatly relieved about because Jim's parents were up there too, and this way he could be on standby if they needed him. Dad, of course, would be safe up at the home.

Late afternoon Ma asked him to run her up to see Dad, figuring it could be a few days before she could get up there again. He didn't know how to say no.

So, he didn't.

"You turn left right up here, son."

"I know, Ma. I used to live here, remember?"

"Oh, you." Ma swatted his arm playfully. "He'll be happy to see you."

He wasn't sure about that; they hadn't left on the best of terms. "Ma, what's going on with him? For real."

"Well," Ma started, and for a second he thought maybe she was going to talk around it, or sugarcoat it or even just flat-out lie. But she dropped that careful expression and looked at him. "He's had two strokes, Scott. I left you messages..."

He nodded. "I knew that, but you'd said he was home."

"Well, he did come home after the second one for a while, but he'd begun having memory problems even before the first one. He'd forget little things at first, but they got..." She shook her head and took a breath. "I tried to help him, I tried in-home help. We tried a couple of different medications but..." Ma cut herself off again, and this time he knew she was fighting back tears. "One night we were sitting in the living room, and he forgot we'd eaten dinner already, just an hour earlier. He shouted at me and he accused me of trying to starve him to death and—honestly, the idea that I would—" Ma pulled a handkerchief out of her purse to dab at her eyes as he put the car in park. "He...he flipped over the coffee table. He shouted in my face, Scott. Your sweet, quiet father just turned into this...thing. If Jim hadn't come in when he did..."

"Oh, Ma." Thank God for Jim. He rested a hand on her knee. "You did the right thing, moving him in here."

Her shoulders sagged. "I hate it. I didn't want to, but Jim and Kate insisted and now...well, now I suppose I can see how right they were, but I still hate it."

He gave her a second to collect herself, and he got out and went around to her side of the car to get the door.

"I'm so glad you're home, son. Your dad is too, I know he is. No matter what, I promise you, he is."

He nodded and let her believe that. This was hard enough on her.

He followed her into a huge atrium entryway that looked more like a hotel lobby than a nursing facility. They signed in at the front desk and Ma led the way to Dad's room, up an elevator, and down a long hallway.

"Hello, Ned." Mom smiled as they went in and Scott saw Dad smile back at her, but it disappeared as soon as Dad looked at him.

"Well, look who's finally home. You punk."

"Ned!"

"Dad—"

"What brings you home, kid? Did you lose your fancy job? What makes you think I have any interest in seeing— seeing you." Dad started to cough.

"Ned. Oh, Ned, where's your water? I'm going to get you some more. Be nice now, Scott's only here for a few days."

As soon as Ma left the room, Dad waved him over.

He went, warily, stopping by the side of his father's bed.

"Listen to me. You want to make this right, you stay home. Your mother needs you. I'm sick, Scott. Sicker than she's going to admit to you. I know it. I don't remember things. I might forget...I might forget her. You. Everything."

Jesus. Dad looked so serious and he thought maybe a little scared. "Everything?"

Dad's hand shot out and caught his arm, squeezing hard. "Take care of your mother."

"Dad—"

"Promise me, Scott." Dad squeezed harder, fingers digging into his arm. "Jarlath is a good kid, but he'll never be you. Promise me you will stay here, stay home and take care of her."

He stared at his father. This man, the one who was talking to him right now, was a hundred percent in control of his faculties. Scott wanted to say yes, but he didn't know if he could—

"Promise me, son!" Dad shouted at him, and he found himself nodding furiously.

"Yeah. Yes. I promise, Dad. I promise."

His dad held his gaze another long moment, finally easing up on his grip. "Good. You're a good boy. I'm still mad at you, but you're a good boy."

"He is, isn't he?" Ma came back to the room with a little pitcher and held a cup with a straw in it up for Dad to drink from.

Dad drank dutifully. "Thank you, dear."

"You look agitated, Ned. Are you not sleeping again?"

"I'm fine, Mother." Dad rolled his eyes at Ma. "Scott was just telling me he has plans to stay in town after all."

He sighed. Well, that was that. He was really home for good. Dad had said it out loud, and to Ma, so it was real.

"Oh! Scott, I'm so pleased. When did you decide that? You're welcome to stay at the house. Are you going to be working at the pub with Jarlath? I heard you were a big help with the Labor Day crowd."

"Oh, I don't know yet, Ma. I'm taking it one day at a time, you know?" One minute at a time, if he was honest. His plans had already changed in the five minutes they'd been here.

Dad sighed and his eyes closed. Ma took his hand and kissed it. "Poor man tires out so quickly. You watch, he'll wake up in a moment." Ma put the water down and fussed over Dad a bit, fixing his blankets and his hair, hanging up a bathrobe. "I'm so glad you're staying in town, son. I've—"

"Who the hell are you?"

He looked over his shoulder at Dad. "It's me, Dad. Scott."

"Scott? Like hell. That punk is in San Francisco."

"It's me, Dad. We just talked about how I was staying in town. Remember?"

Dad looked horrified for a second and when that expression disappeared, the rest of him disappeared too, and suddenly it didn't matter who he was anymore. Dad started complaining about the hard bed, some nurse that he didn't care for, and a roommate who had apparently moved out weeks ago.

They stayed long enough for Ma to feed Dad dinner; then they left. Ma cried all the way home. "At least he remembered you," she'd said as if calling him a punk was something to celebrate. He didn't know how to feel about any of it.

He went to bed still processing everything. He needed to tell the moving company that was storing his belongings to send them here. He needed to find another job. And he had to talk to Jarlath and find out what Ma wasn't telling him about Dad.

He eventually gave up trying to sleep. After getting a snack and flipping channels on TV, he wandered out to the garage and dug out his old motorcycle. He spent the night cleaning it, tuning up the engine and inflating the tires. If he was staying in town, he needed wheels, right?

Dad hated his motorcycle, but they'd kept it for him anyway, hadn't they? He and Dad had been like oil and water but when it came down to brass tacks, Dad had trusted him enough to ask him to look after Ma.

Jarlath is a good kid, but he'll never be you.

God. Why were relationships with parents so complicated?

Scott worked on his bike until the dim predawn hour; then he took it for an early morning ride before the world woke up. He drove it through deserted downtown Falmouth, around the winding streets of the Heights and down to the beach, following the long, coastal roads. He ended up outside O'Connolly's.

Jarlath's truck was parked alone in the lot. Sure, the sun was up now, but it was still damn early to be at work.

Twenty minutes later, he had breakfast sandwiches from Dunkin' and two giant hot coffees. It was a either peace offering or a large shot of caffeinated courage. It was hard to say which it would be until he'd actually seen Jar.

He used the buzzer at the back entrance and waited.

"Hey, Kent. Didn't you get my—*oh.*" Jar opened the door with a cell phone in one hand and rolled his eyes when he realized Scott wasn't a guy named Kent. Jar turned and walked away, putting the phone to his ear and leaving the door wide open.

That meant he should go in, right? So he did, then closed the door behind him.

"I've got a big delivery of sandbags coming at ten. I just need some help getting Dad's shutters up and stacking furniture and stuff....Will you?...That would be great, thanks so much, man....Yeah. Grinders on me later, and all the cold beer you can carry out, right?...We're probably going to lose power anyway. See you soon."

He followed Jar out to the bar, which was covered in tools on one end and paperwork on the other. "Jim's on his way. Ezra's going to make some calls and bring some more folks with him. I need—"

"Coffee." Scott set one down in front of Jar, and Jar

picked it up without missing a beat and sipped it.

Jar looked at him and nodded his thanks. "We have to talk, but I don't have time. I do need all the hands I can get right now, though, and I appreciate you being here."

Scott set an egg sandwich down for Jar, took a seat, and opened his up.

"I appreciate the breakfast too, I didn't even think about food when I left the house this morning. Thanks."

"You never did." Jar had always been skinny, that was his default, but he'd also been the kid that forgot to eat. Scott didn't understand people that forgot to eat; sometimes his day was literally one meal to the next.

Jar shrugged. "Guess that's true."

They ate quietly for a bit, both of them hungry and chewing, and sipped their coffee. They did have things to talk about, though Scott didn't think any of it would be as big as Jar seemed to. Regardless, Jar was right, he had enough on his plate today.

Jim let himself in. "Just me, Jarlath," he called from the back of house.

"Hey, Jim." Jar crumpled up his breakfast wrapper and pitched it, then stuck out a hand to Jim. "Thanks for coming."

Jim shook it, grinning. "I heard there was going to be free beer so..."

"Uh-huh. Well, that's the rumor."

Jim looked around. "Where are we starting?"

"Down cellar." Jar held up one finger, took one more big swig of his coffee, then headed for the cellar door. "You guys okay with carrying? No back problems?"

Jim snorted. "Jesus, Jarlath. I'm not that old yet."

They all laughed.

"Okay. The shutters are there, they all have to come up

and can be put right out front. Not against the pub, though; we'll stack them on the sidewalk." Jar pointed, giving them the lay of the land. "The pallets are for inside, we'll stack chairs and tables on top of them in case we flood, they'll at least have a chance of staying dry. And those make a plywood cover for the bar. Dad always put the bar appliances and stuff up on top of the bar cover to keep them dry."

He nodded. Some of this he remembered.

"We'll get a start, but when more people get here, can one of you hang out down here to direct them?"

"Yeah. I can do that." Jim raised a finger, volunteering. Scott was fine with that.

"Works for me."

"Okay. Perfect." Jar looked at him. "Do you remember the sandbag routine?"

"Yeah, I got it. You're not building a barrier, are you?"

"No. There's no point. If it comes up over the sea wall, that's pretty much it."

They'd need a couple of thousand sandbags to build a decent barrier around the pub, and resources like that just weren't available. They'd do what they could to protect the foundation, block the doors, and keep water out of the building, but Jar was right, if the water made it over the seawall, which was just across the street, there'd be no stopping it.

"Okay. I can do sandbag duty."

"Great. Perfect." Jar looked between him and Jim. "This sucks."

"Boss? I got a few people here." That sounded like Ezra.

"Hey, Ezra, be right up." Jar grabbed a pallet and started up the stairs.

"Have you seen the forecast?"

"Yeah," Jim shook his head. "There's no telling yet. It looks bad, but it could shift by tonight. I hate that it's coming in after dark, though." Jim grabbed a pallet, and he followed suit.

An hour later, Scott was out on the sidewalk, stacking sandbags with a small crew of extended family. Ironically, it was a gorgeous day. A little windy, but the sun was shining.

"Beautiful day to be stacking sandbags," he joked.

"Right?" His cousin Ken laughed.

"You all boarded up?" Dad's side of the family had beachfront property.

"Yeah, everyone's moved up to Aunt Julie's house until the storm is over."

"Good call." He didn't know an Aunt Julie; that must be someone on Ken's mother's side.

"Man, between that and this I'm gonna be sore tomorrow."

"Yeah, well...I hope I'm sore but drinking a beer here Thursday night, bitching about how we did all of this for nothing."

Ken agreed, nodding. "Best-case scenario, right?"

"You know it." It was as likely as not at this point, so he'd take it.

His crew stacked six pickups' worth of sandbags around all the doors and the front foundation, and eventually the trucks of sandbags stopped coming, so he figured that was their lot.

Jarlath came out just as they were finishing up. "Grinders inside guys, and beer."

Ken grinned. "I'm here for the beer." *Heeyah fah the beeyah.*

Scott laughed a shook his head. Townies. Some things never changed—and he was glad for that.

9

Jarlath had fifteen people in his pub eating and drinking, mostly on the floor because the tables and chairs were already stacked off the ground and secured. While they were all inside, he went outside, technically to have a look at the sandbag situation, but really it was just to get some air.

Fuck, this was nerve-wracking. The forecast was evolving, and it was starting to look worse for the Cape, not better. No amount of insurance was going to make him less nervous. The pub was his baby. Hell, it was basically his birthright. He'd grown up playing in Dad's office, then bussing tables, serving food, and finally working behind the bar. In a lot of ways, it was home. He'd lost his first tooth in Dad's office. His first kiss was with a girl named Samantha in the parking lot.

He'd kissed his first boy in the cellar.

That boy was Scotty Borden.

And after that kiss, he'd finally understood who he was, and he'd never kissed a girl again. For the rest of high school, it had been Scott and no one else.

He looked the sandbags over and of course they looked great; this wasn't Scott's first hurricane at the bar. Hurricanes were something else they'd grown up with.

He thought it had only been Scott because there was pretty much no one else. But he'd missed Scott for real when Scott left for the west coast. For real, meaning more than someone missed a best friend. His heart had ached. It had hurt so bad he'd cried a couple of times. It hadn't taken him long to understand what Scott had really been to him.

He sighed and shook his head. He didn't have time to be thinking about ghosts and memories. He had a fuckload of *right now* to deal with.

Kate wandered out, clearly looking for him. "Are you gonna eat, Jar?"

He puffed out a breath. He could let his hair down a little around Kate; she was as close to a sister as he'd ever get. "I don't know. My stomach is in knots."

"Yeah. I bet it is." She took his hand and held it, looking at him kindly, which didn't make him feel any less anxious.

"What?"

"Well, let's go over this. You'll be here late, as late as you can with the weather, then you'll go home—"

"Maybe. I might stay here."

"Stay here? Why?"

"In case...you know." He shrugged, knowing it was a bad idea.

"What are you going to do, Jar? Stand out front and yell at the ocean to back off?"

He looked at the sky. "No. No, I know."

"If the water comes in, there's no stopping it. There's no saving anything you haven't already gotten off the ground or put in your truck."

"I know...I know, Kate." God, he hated feeling helpless, though.

"So you'll go home...promise." She gave him a meaningful look.

"I'll go home. I promise."

"And then what? You won't sleep, so you'll be up all night, likely without power, and you'll be back here the minute it's safe for you to drive. Sound about right?"

He nodded. "Yep."

"So, you'll need energy, strength...food, Jar. Food."

"Kate—"

"Shut up and come eat."

"Yes, ma'am." He let her lead him inside. He hadn't been through the door a minute when someone cleared off a barstool and gave him a sandwich and a beer.

"I don't know how to thank everybody."

Kate rubbed his back. "Keep running the best, friendliest pub in town."

"That doesn't seem like enough." Nothing did.

Ezra leaned on the bar with him. "It's not. But they don't care. They're going to go home talking about how cool it was that you fed them, and they'll all have beer for the storm. It's fine, Boss."

He nodded. It was about the best he could do, anyway. "We'll get the bar covered and the appliances up after we eat and let everyone raid the walk-ins."

"Sounds good. Don't stress it, Boss, they all know how worried you are."

He snorted at that, but what was he going to say? He was worried. But at least he wasn't worried about his people. The locals were old hats at this gig. Buildings were less important than people.

Even Dad's pub.

———

By DUSK, the wind was picking up and Jar could smell the storm coming—ozone and salty spray—and the little hairs on his arms were standing up.

Jesus, this was going to be a bad one. He just knew it. Everyone did.

"I'm going home, Boss. You should too." Ezra gave him a pat on the shoulder. "How about I walk you out?"

He started to protest. He wasn't ready yet, but he wasn't going to be any more ready an hour from now, and it would just be a tougher drive. "Yeah. Okay."

"Scott? You ready?"

Scott was still here?

"Guess so. It's not getting better out there. Come on, Jar."

Jar grabbed the last box of essentials from the office—the laptop, the last of the important paperwork, the cash from the safe, and his bottle of Bushmills 21 from Dad's desk. "Coming."

The sky was green, the wind was blowing, and there were only two vehicles in the parking lot.

"Hop in, Scott." Ezra unlocked the doors to his Nissan and headed for the driver's side.

Jar looked around. "Where's your bike?"

"Jim rode it back to Ma's for me. It's no good in this weather."

"Oh. Yeah, good call." Jar looked at Scott for a long moment. "How about I drive you? It's more on the way. Ezra's headed up to his in-laws."

"Oh. yeah? I thought—you don't mind?"

"Time to go, Scott!" Ezra called over the wind.

"Jar's got me. Thanks, man. Be safe!"

Ezra nodded and gave them a thumbs-up. "You too. Stay in touch, Boss."

Jarlath gave Ezra a thumbs-up in return so he didn't have to shout over the wind. They'd be texting on and off all night. Ezra was as invested as he was; the bar was Ezra's livelihood. It was how he supported his family.

They watched Ezra's truck drive off. "Okay, let's roll." Jarlath unlocked the doors and they climbed in quickly. "Man. This is picking up fast."

"You sure you want to go home alone, Jar? You could stay with us. Ma would probably love that."

The last thing he needed was to have to watch his p's and q's around Ma while he was stressed and not sleeping. "Yeah. I've got neighbors and, you know, we look out for each other. I'll be okay." Jar took off fast, though, not wasting a second of time.

"I know you'll be safe. That's not what I—"

"Look, I'm fine. I just need to get to the other side of this. I hate not knowing. I mean, I want everything to be okay, but if I just knew it wasn't going to be I could sleep." He shrugged. "I guess that sounds stupid."

"You can't control everything."

"I know. And that's a fascinating comment coming from you." It was a crappy thing to say and when Scott didn't respond, he realized just how much. "I'm sorry. I'm in a shit mood right now, I need to just shut my mouth."

Scott nodded. "No worries."

Jarlath sighed. "I'm glad you're here to look after Ma."

"For once, right?" Scott crossed his arms over his chest.

"I didn't say that."

"No, you didn't need to. Everyone else is. And they've all pointed out how you stepped up while I was gone. Even Jim."

He sighed. He didn't do it to make Scott look bad, he did it because he loved them. "Fuck, I'm sorry."

"Don't be. Ma needed you. Dad too." Scott glanced over at him. "But I'm staying now."

Whoa, what? "You're staying?"

Scott nodded. "I promised Dad I would."

He didn't know what to say. But Ned missed Scott a lot. More than Scott probably understood, but that conversation was going to have to wait. Jarlath pulled into Ma's driveway. "Keep in touch tonight?"

"Yeah. You too. I'm going to worry about you." Scott rested a hand on his knee, startling him, the touch so hot he thought it might burn right into his skin.

"Yeah." He could hardly meet Scott's eyes. "I'll be up."

"Talk soon." Scott looked at the house, took a breath, and ran for it.

Jar waited until Scott was safely inside to drive off, then made his way home. This time he didn't go over the Green Pond bridge; it seemed safer to go home on a more inland road. The marina guys had taken his boat off her mooring and put her in a slip for him where she'd be safer. It had cost him a little, but it was worth it. A big storm could rip a boat off its mooring—he'd seen boats end up on the jetties or the rocks supporting the bridge. He'd also seen boats drag their moorings ten or fifteen yards.

Wind and water were no joke.

That hand on his knee was no joke either. And now Scott was staying in town?

The things he had no goddamn control over were piling up. Scott Borden and a hurricane in the same fucking week? The weather was bad, but Scott's sudden reappearance was a close second.

When he pulled into his sandy driveway, the wind was

blowing the cape pines in the yard sideways and the rain was starting. Huge drops that pelted him as he hurried into the house. God, he'd been so focused on the pub, he hadn't done much of anything at the house. It was high enough up that it wouldn't flood, but he had furniture out back and stuff on the screen porch.

He rushed around, dragging things onto the porch and stacking them against the house. The last thing he did before he went inside for good was lock the screen door and tie the handle to a heavy hook so it wouldn't fly open. That was why the hook was there; Dad had put it in when Jarlath was a kid.

He hauled out his lantern and a flashlight, a charger for his phone, and got himself a beer. He'd watch a movie until the lights went out. Then maybe he'd try to sleep.

He snorted a laugh as he opened his beer. He wasn't going to sleep.

He had his pub to think about.

And a man too.

10

Around nine o'clock, Scott got Ma all tucked in. "You have a flashlight right here, Ma."

"Thank you, son."

"And your phone is plugged in, okay?"

"I appreciate that."

He lingered in her doorway. "So...you're good?"

"I'm fine, dear." Ma tilted her head. "How are you?"

"I'm fine." He shrugged. He wasn't fine, but he wasn't sure why.

"Scotty. This house was built in the fifties. Everyone said your grandfather was crazy to not build right on the beach, but he knew better. He picked out a perfect location, and we've been just fine here. We were fine my whole life, and yours too. This house even made it through Hurricane Bob, when a lot of people were struggling. It will make it through this one too."

"I know, Ma. It's not the house."

Ma gave him a knowing look. "Just remember, son, people are more important than pubs."

He shrugged. "You think Pop O'Connolly would have said that?"

"I know he would have." She nodded once, absolutely sure. "He would fret and pace just like Jarlath is probably doing right now, and when the storm was gone, he was always grateful that everyone he loved was okay. He just went on about whatever he needed to do to get back in business."

She was right. He didn't remember Hurricane Bob, but he knew it had wrecked the pub. There were pictures of before, during, and after the rebuild on the walls in the office at O'Connolly's. Jar's dad had been proud of them.

"You go to sleep, son. Or don't, and give Jarlath a call. He's alone in that house, after all."

"I tried to get him to stay here."

"Oh, that's his parents' house," Ma said sagely. "The pub may feel like home, but it isn't."

"True that. I'll call."

"And then sleep." She nodded her approval. "I'm going to. It's just noise when everything is dark. Nothing to see." She leaned over and turned out her light.

Nothing to see. It must be good to be almost seventy and just *know* things like Ma did.

"Night, Ma."

"Night, Scotty."

He closed her door and shuffled into the kitchen to make coffee, only to find that Ma already had and there was a fresh pot waiting for him. She really did know things. He poured a cup and took two cookies out of Ma's cookie jar. Oatmeal raisin, his favorite, and she'd be happy to see the jar half-empty.

He pulled out his phone and texted Jar, figuring he wouldn't call in case Jar had tried to doze off. *Blowy out there.*

Yup. Wish I could see better. Jar hadn't dozed off; that reply came back in seconds.

Ma says there's nothing to see.

That's Ma. Solid as a rock.

She went to bed. I think she thought I was fussing too much.

Glad she's good. All good here too. Dock is high, but not bad. Not going to worry unless something hits the house.

Okay. Try to sleep. He knew that wasn't going to happen.

You too.

Scott dropped his phone back into his pocket and went up to his room. He turned on the TV and flipped channels, deliberately avoiding the news. He was getting enough information from the alerts on his phone.

One of those alerts woke Scott and he blinked at his phone. He must have dozed off watching TV. It was just after two a.m.

Lacey at the marina says they're taking a beating.

He rubbed his eyes to clear them and read Jar's next text too.

Cat 4. Ben at the fire station says power's out in the Heights.

That meant the power was out at the pub, but Jar had expected that. Category 4? Shit, he expected they'd lose power too before long.

Is the Jenny okay? The *Jenny* was Jar's sailboat. Jar had bought her second or maybe third hand after graduation and shined her up. He'd spent every dollar he made on her for a year.

They don't know. She was still in the slip last I heard.

Good place for her. You okay?

I'm good. Starting to get anxious.

Starting to? Jar had been anxious for days. *Breathe. How's the house?*

Jar didn't reply right away, but he saw those three dots

going at the bottom of his screen. A couple of minutes later, Jar sent, *I just lost power.*

And, as if Jar had made it happen by saying it out loud, he lost power too. *Me too. Just now.*

Gonna light candles and save my phone battery.

Okay, be safe.

You too.

Scott sighed and looked around his dark bedroom. Why was it that when the lights went out, everything seemed louder? He slid out of bed, went down to the kitchen to put the rest of the coffee in a travel mug so it wouldn't get cold, and grabbed a couple of cookies. Then he went back upstairs, where he fell asleep again.

When he woke up the next time it was still raining but not nearly as hard, and the wind had died down a lot too, but the dawn sky was still that weird green. He peered out his bedroom window at the debris in the front yard—some branches and a lot of leaves, a garbage can lid, something metal that looked like it might be a chimney cap. Hopefully not theirs, but he'd get up on the roof and look when the rain stopped.

He grabbed his phone but didn't see an update from Jar. *Hrm.* Was that a good thing or bad?

He pulled on a robe and headed downstairs.

Ma had obviously been up, though she wasn't in the kitchen. They still didn't have power, but she'd put cereal and milk out on the counter—*Only open the fridge once, dear* —along with a carton of juice and some blueberry muffins. Homemade, of course. She'd baked them while everyone was out boarding things up so they'd have breakfast if the power went out.

There was also a little jar of instant coffee, a box of kitchen matches, and a kettle on the gas stove.

Jar was right, Ma really was solid.

He put a perfectly good breakfast together despite the lack of power and pulled up the news app on his phone.

"Hurricane Eric first made landfall Wednesday afternoon on Block Island as a category two and grew quickly to a category three as it moved north, with strong winds and heavy rainfall causing serious damage."

"Oh, is that the news, Scotty?" Mom wandered in with a mug in her hands and sat with him.

"Yeah, Ma. Shhh."

"...a wind gust of a hundred and thirty miles per hour was recorded at one high school there before the anemometer blew away."

Wow.

"Whoopsie." Mom giggled softly.

"On Cape Cod, the town of Falmouth reported gusts of a hundred and fifty miles per hour. The tidal surge was over ten feet above normal and coastal damage in and around Falmouth Harbor was devastating in places due to the wind and the high waves."

"Oh..." Ma put a hand on his shoulder.

"Jesus Christ." His first thought was how the hell had he slept through all of that. But his next one was, *Jarlath.*

Ma was on the same wavelength. "Have you called him?"

"Not yet. When the lights went out, he said he was turning off his phone to save the battery."

"Ah." Ma nodded, but she was giving him that look.

"I should call." He said quickly, then closed the news app and dialed.

"Mm." Ma approved.

The phone rang. And rang. And rang. And—

"Hey, Scott. I can't get there." Jarlath's voice was hoarse, almost like he'd been yelling. "I tried, I went toward the harbor but the bridge is closed. I went around the long way but the hill over the heights is blocked by trees, and even through town half the roads have barricades and...it's a mess."

He sighed. "Fuck."

"It's a fucking mess."

Wait, Jar was out? "Where are you now?"

"I'm...uh. Home. I'm in my truck."

Okay. Jar needed to get to the pub, he understood. "Can you make it here?"

"I don't know. I have a tree down—it missed the house. The floating dock is way high, but we didn't flood. Yet." Jar sighed again.

"All right. I'm going to loop around the other way and see if I can find a clear way through. Can you walk over the bridge? Maybe I can pick you up on the other side." That could actually work.

"You...yeah?"

"Yeah. We don't have power, I'm just sitting here."

"Okay. Okay, great." Jar sounded relieved. "Call me if you can get there?"

"I will. I'll need some time."

"I've got plenty."

"Hang tight, Jar. I'll call you."

"Thanks. Thanks a lot."

"Talk soon." He hung up the phone with another sigh, this one heavier than the last.

Ma was right there, rubbing his back like she had the night they'd lost the big football match his senior year. "You're a good friend, son."

He shrugged. "I better get dressed."

He hadn't been much of a friend recently, but he had a chance to be now.

Assuming he could get there.

11

The *Jenny looks good.* Lacey's text came in right after Jarlath hung up with Scott.

Okay. Some good news. *Thank you! Are you okay?*

We've got a mess. Boats on the jetty. The Blue Madame is on the bridge.

Jarlath hit dial and called Lacey.

"Yes, I said *on* the bridge."

"Shit. Is that why it's closed?"

"Yup."

"Can I still walk across it?"

"Oh, yeah. You just can't get a car around her. And I bet they don't get here to help us move her until tomorrow."

"I have to check on the pub but if it's okay, I'll come out tomorrow."

Lacey sighed. "I'll keep my fingers crossed, Jar. But—"

"I know. I heard." The Heights were a mess.

"Fingers crossed. We'll get your *Jenny* back on her mooring as soon as it's safe. She looks good."

"Thanks so much, Lacey. Be careful."

"You too, Jar. Bye now." She hung up first.

He took a deep breath and texted Scott. *I can get over the bridge.*

Start walking. I just made it.

Yes! He just needed to see the pub. Whatever it was, no matter how bad, he just needed to know so he could decide what to do next. He couldn't sit here worrying and doing nothing anymore. His dad always said worrying was a waste of energy. Do, or don't do.

OMW. He texted Scott back and put the truck in gear.

Jar glanced one more time at the tree in his yard. It was down but harmless where it was, just lying there. He could deal with it later. He put his truck in gear and drove toward the bridge, moving slowly through his neighborhood which, all things considered, could have been in much worse shape.

He parked his truck as close as the orange cones allowed and walked around the last corner to the bridge, eyes going wide when he saw her. The *Blue Madame* was up on the bridge all right, but from this angle she looked strangely fine otherwise. As he walked past her, he caught some bumps and scrapes, but mostly it seemed as if the waves had just lifted her up and sat her down there.

Crazy.

"Jar!" Scott waved at him from the far side of the bridge.

He waved back and made his way over. "Hey. Thank you so much for doing this."

"It was easier to get here than I expected." Scott held out a coffee. "It's hot. The fish market has a generator."

"I owe you. Thanks, man. Did you get to the pub?"

"Not yet. I figured we'd put our heads together on that one. I was told Grand Ave is mostly washed out."

"Fuck." That meant water. He sighed. "Okay. The long way...uh, twenty-eight over to Worchester?"

"*Woostah*," Scott said with a toothy grin, pronouncing the name the salty Cape Cod way.

"God, you sound just like Dad."

Scott laughed and the sound was soothing in a weird way. Jarlath had to fight the urge to hug him for all of this.

"I got Ma's muffins in the car."

"Blueberry?"

"You know it. Only the best for a hurricane." Scott climbed into Ma's sensible sedan. "Sorry, it's not as sexy as your truck."

"Or as hot as your bike."

That earned him a big grin. "The bike *is* hot, right?"

"A little." *A lot.* Scott could keep smiling like that. He needed smiles right now, and he'd missed that one.

Scott chuckled and turned on the radio as they drove off.

The inland route was even longer with traffic and a couple of detours, but the rain and the wind had let up by the time they headed down Worchester and back toward the beach. He was feeling a little steadier too—they were full of muffins and coffee, and he was enjoying listening to Scott sing along with the radio.

He couldn't quite do it; he was still anxious about the pub. But he'd be lying if he didn't admit he appreciated Scott for being here, and even for trying to lighten the mood.

"Tree." The car rolled to a stop just up the road from the pub.

"Hm." He took off his seat belt and opened the car door to have a look. He saw the tree, but it was what was in the road beyond it that really caught his eye.

"Jar, what is that?" Scott got out of the car too.

"That looks like a piling from the beachfront deck at the

Wharf." He could tell by the light fixture on the top, which was beat-up but recognizable.

"Jesus."

Yeah. That was something else. "You want to walk?"

"I think we better. I don't want to give Ma a flat." Scott got back in, drove the car off to the shoulder, and parked it. "Okay. Let's go."

"Scott. That seriously came up from the beach?" That meant the water had been up this far at some point. "Fuck." The pub could totally be toast.

"Yeah. I wonder if the water brought that tree down too, not the wind. Keep breathing." Scott led the way, weaving around bits of dock and other debris. Then, just as the pub came into view, so did the water.

Jarlath shuffled to a stop. "Well. It's wet."

"But it's standing." Scott put a hand on his shoulder.

"Yep." He stared at it, doing a mental inventory of what he was seeing and what it meant. The pub, the house behind it, and the little inn next door were all under water. It was hard to tell how much, but he could only see the very tops of the sandbags. He sighed.

"Might not be safe to—"

"Then you can stay here." Jarlath marched his way over until he couldn't march anymore and had to wade instead. He couldn't see in any of the windows because they'd boarded them up. They were wet, though; the water had been a good foot and a half or so higher at one point. Which meant the sandbags had been underwater too.

"You think the water got in?"

"Probably. Yeah. I think so. But before I open a door..."

"Hang on. I'll be right back." Scott hurried off to the car.

The water was nearly knee-deep, but it was possible they were holding some of it off now.

"Crowbar." Scott brought that and a box of tools with him.

"Perfect. Jesus, Scott. Thanks for thinking about it."

"Ma," Scott said with a shrug.

He shook his head and even let himself grin a little. She was old Cape, for sure. He pried the shutter off the upper half of the side door and handed it to Scott. He peered into the dark pub. "I can't see."

"Um...I have a big lantern flashlight. In this bag." Scott held the bag out with one hand and Jarlath dug through it.

"Thanks." He shone the light inside and it took him no time at all to see the water, standing just as high as it was outside. "Yeah, it's flooded." The sight of all that water...it was all over the bar...it had to be six or eight inches deep.

Fuck.

"What do you want to do?"

"I don't know. Let's take a walk around the outside?" He was dreading this, but he needed to know. He steeled himself and started walking.

"Mhm." Scott set the shutter down on top of the sandbags and followed him.

From the front, the outside actually looked okay. He waded out into the street a bit and looked up. "Some missing shingles over here. Roof looks okay, though." The inn's roof and porch looked good too. Wet sucked, but it didn't look like either of them was going to need a new roof.

"Lucky."

"Very." *Thank God.* One less thing to worry about.

"Well, that's something. You want to go inside?"

"I'm going to call Daisy about the inn and let her know what's going on. And then..." He sighed. "Honestly, there's no point in going inside yet. Everything is up higher than the water level is right now, so there's really nothing to do. I bet Dad's desk is toast, though." The desk, the chair, but maybe not the rug—they'd put that up higher. The pictures should be okay too, unless the place shook bad enough to knock them off the walls.

He was going to miss that desk. It had been there for as long as he could remember. It reminded him of Dad when he sat there.

Scott nodded. "Yeah, maybe."

He took a breath. Water was bad, but he could fix this. His incredibly expensive insurance would help. Floors, the bar, the walk-ins, the bathrooms...but the building seemed solid, and the shutters had held, so hopefully most of the windows behind them were okay. He had a lot of windows.

So that was that. "Take me home."

"Jar, maybe you should—"

"Scott. I have a tree to cut up before sundown." He needed to do something constructive. He was going to get that tree done so tomorrow he could focus on this. Assuming the water had receded by then.

"Right. Come on. I'll help."

He glanced at Scott. He was tired. Exhausted actually, and he could use the help. He was going to owe Scott big-time after this. He nodded and followed Scott back up the road to the car.

"Hey, the tide is going out fast, Jar. The water was up to here when we got here."

Scott was right, it had receded a little even in the short time they'd been here. "That's good. I'll be able to get inside tomorrow."

He called Daisy from the car, and she was grateful to hear from him. She hadn't been able to get down to the inn either; she had issues with her mom's house to deal with. But at least she'd sleep better tonight.

Maybe. He wasn't sure he would sleep better. Maybe chopping up that tree would wear him out enough that he wouldn't really have a choice.

They parked the car at the fish market on one side of the bridge and walked across it, past the boat still blocking the road, to the marina where Jarlath had left his truck. There was a crew arriving and a crane in the marina parking lot. He crossed his fingers for the *Blue Madame*. He thought he could see his *Jenny* sitting in her slip from the bridge, but he wasn't sure. He'd check on her soon.

They took his truck home. His neighbors were all out, and one of them waved him over. He rolled down his window. "Heya, Ben."

"Did you get to your place, Jar?"

"Yep. It's wet, but it could be worse. You good?"

Ben nodded. "We've got power back already. Nobody on your side flooded. This was a bad one, but we're okay. Just cleaning up the yard."

"Has anyone checked in on Mrs. Silva?"

"Her son came by, she's fine. Martha's bringing her dinner. She's worried about you, though. You should stop in and say hello."

"I will. Just have to clear a tree."

"Don't let me keep you. Sorry about the water, I hope it's not too bad."

"Thanks, Ben. Talk soon." Jarlath drove two more houses down and pulled into his driveway.

"Mrs. Silva's still hanging in there, huh?" Scott jumped out of the truck.

"You know it. She's ninety-eight now, she can't get out of the house by herself, but she's doing great. Remembers everything." Which is why he would go see her soon. She'd remember if he didn't.

"Just the one tree?"

"Yeah. I lucked out, this wasn't even a close call."

"You have a chainsaw?"

"In the shed, which is also still standing." The shed was mostly cinderblock. His father had built it to last, and it wasn't going anywhere.

"All right. I'll get it, you check on the house now that the power's back up." Scott smiled again, catching him with those blue eyes and Jarlath had to force himself to breathe. He could do this. He could have done this by himself, but Scott was here and taking charge and he couldn't bring himself to argue.

Jarlath stepped up; it was what he did. Any time he was needed, he was there. Every little problem at the pub, he'd figured it out. But Scott was stepping up for him right now, and he promised himself it was okay. It was okay to accept some help. It was okay to need it. Even from Scott.

"Jar?"

"S...sorry I...um. I'll check on the house." No, his hands were not shaking. He was fine.

"You okay?" Scott rested a hand on his shoulder.

He nodded. That touch. He panicked a little, afraid he couldn't handle it. *Fuck.* He'd kept it together this long; he was stronger than this, wasn't he? "Yeah. I'll be right back." He could feel Scott's eyes on him as he went into the house. *Breathe. Get the tree taken care of and send Scott home. Then you can lose it.*

He took a deep breath and looked around inside before going around and shutting off lights he didn't need. Away from Scott, things were easier. He could think. He had this. He'd make some coffee and get to work.

12

Scott hadn't used a chainsaw in years, and he was surprised how good it felt to be outdoors, doing some real physical work. Meaningful work, not just a workout. He cut and chopped and dismantled, and Jar stacked the good pieces for firewood and gathered the smaller ones for kindling. In the end, a fallen tree turned out to be a good thing. Jar had a nice stash of wood for his firepit, and some of it might even last into colder weather.

But Jar looked exhausted. Just completely wrung out.

"You want a sandwich? I didn't open the fridge and the power wasn't out that long, I bet stuff is okay."

"Sure. Sounds great. I'll stack this last bit."

"I can help finish up."

"No, it's cool. I—*ow!*" He and Jar reached down for the last few logs at the same time and cracked their heads together like a couple of idiots. He squeezed his eyes closed, and the flash of headache went away quickly. "Fuck." He laughed, feeling stupid. "Damn."

Jar was quiet, though, rubbing his head.

Shit.

"Hey. You okay?" He caught Jar's shoulder with one hand.

"Oh, yeah." Jar sighed and straightened up, pinning him with a stare from those endlessly deep brown eyes. "Sure. I'm fine. My dad's pub is underwater, I didn't sleep last night, and this tree is fucking pissing me off, but yeah. I'm totally fine, Scott! Totally fucking *fine!*" Jar tossed the log he'd picked up to the ground, turned around and went into the house, letting the screen door slam behind him.

Well, fuck.

Scott decided not to follow. Not yet, anyway. Jar was stressed and exhausted and probably needed a minute to breathe. Instead, he bent again, gathered up the last of the wood, and stacked it neatly on the pile in the lean-to-style storage rack behind the house. He stopped at the top of the little hill down to Jar's dock after putting the chainsaw away and looked out over the pond. Jar was right—the water was crazy; he couldn't remember ever seeing the dock float so high. But with the hill, the houses along here weren't in any danger of flooding.

Trees, though? They were a problem. He could hear other chainsaws going down the road.

Okay, sooner or later he was going to have to go inside and check on Jar without looking like he was...well, checking on Jar. He took a breath and headed for the back door.

Jar was in the kitchen, leaning against the counter and sipping what Scott assumed was a cup of coffee from a mug with his name on it. He glanced up as Scott moved toward him and sighed heavily.

"I'm sorry."

"You've had the mother of all bad days, don't even worry

about it." He stepped closer, thinking he'd give Jar a hug if Jar would let him.

"It has sucked a little." Jar looked down at his mug again, holding it like he was warming his fingers. "Still—"

"Don't."

"I shouldn't have taken it out on you."

"Jar." When he was close enough, he reached out, catching Jar lightly by one elbow.

Jar didn't look up, but he leaned forward and dropped his forehead against Scott's shoulder.

Oh. He slid his other hand across Jar's back and rested it on Jar's nape, and when all Jar did was sigh and didn't protest, Scott turned his head and nuzzled gently, just the tiniest bit, into Jar's dark hair. Jar smelled like sweat and musk, different than he used to, older, more like a man and less like teenage lust.

He broke out in goose bumps despite feeling suddenly warm. "Jar," he whispered.

Jar shook his head, pressing it deeper into his shoulder. "We need to talk, huh?"

Patti Page started singing "Old Cape Cod" and Jar took a sudden, sharp breath, pushing away from him. "Oh. That's Ma."

Oh, come on, Ma! He cursed his mother's timing.

Jar exhaled and grabbed his phone off the counter, clearing his throat before answering. "Hey, Ma." Jar set his coffee down. "I'm okay....We did get there. The pub is standing in about a foot of water, but the tide was going out. It looks okay otherwise. I'll know more when I can get in there tomorrow....Yes, he's here." Jar looked at him, and he could read the confusion in those eyes. And the exhaustion. "He's been, uh...helping me. With a tree."

That was truthful. Mostly.

"Still no power, huh? Well, do you—oh, Jim's coming to get you?" Scott thought maybe Jar was repeating things for his benefit now. "That's good, Ma....Oh, no worries, I'll make sure Scott eats and...yeah. Yeah, I'll ask him. Be safe, now. Tell everyone we said hi....Love you too. Bye-bye."

Jar put his phone down on the counter, next to his coffee cup. "Ma doesn't have power yet. She wants you to know she's going to be staying with Kate and Jim."

"Great. Perfect. I'm glad they're okay." And now he could focus on Jar.

"Yeah, she says they're good."

"What did she want you to ask me?"

"Hm?"

Was Jar avoiding the question? "Ma. I heard you tell her you'd ask me something."

"Oh, uh." Jar picked up his mug and turned his back as he headed for the kitchen sink. "She suggested you stay. You know, here. Tonight. Because...because I have power, and she's taking everything from the fridge in a cooler to Kate's." Jar put his mug down. "She asked me to make sure you ate too. Are you hungry?"

He wasn't hungry. "Do you want me to stay?"

Jar blinked at him. "I..."

"Here?" He moved closer, eyes holding Jar's gaze. "With you."

"Well, you don't want to be alone, you know, with no power."

"No. I don't want to be alone." That had nothing to do with the power, though. He stepped in front of Jar, looking down at him. Soaking up Jar's heat. There was no way Jar wasn't feeling this.

"It's not uh...fuck." Jar broke the stare and leaned into

him. The man was trembling. "It's not that I...I just don't... I'm just so fucking tired, Scott."

"I know." He put an arm around Jar's shoulders and Jar leaned harder.

"I'm sorry. I-I'm sorry."

"Don't apologize. This was a fucking shitty day, Jar." A scary day. Jar was dealing with a ton of stress.

"It *was* a shitty day. And I just had to walk away from the pub....I couldn't do anything."

The only time he'd ever seen Jar cry was when his mother died. This was as close as he'd seen Jar since. "You sound like your dad. He never sat still."

Jar snorted. "I keep asking myself what he'd do right now."

That he knew. "Ma told me he'd be grateful the people he loved were okay, and just get on with whatever he needed to do for the pub."

Jar looked up at him. "Ma told you that?"

"She did. I think she's right."

Jar nodded and straightened up. "I think so too. I need to go to bed. Get some sleep." Jar had dark circles under his dark eyes.

"Is the little guest room in the back still—"

Jar stopped him with a hand on his arm. "Stay with me?"

He froze and searched Jar's eyes. "Are you sure?"

Jar nodded. "I don't want to be alone either."

"Then yeah. I'd like that." He smiled as Jar took his hand and led him into— "Wait, this was your parents' room."

Jar snorted. "Seriously? This is a problem for you?"

"No. I mean, kind of. I'm surprised is all. But no. I'm good."

He thought.

No, it was cool. Sure.

"It's a new bed." Jar sat on it to take off his shoes.

"Oh, well, in that case." He sat too, right next to Jar, shoulder to shoulder.

"It beats me staying with you," Jar teased.

"Oh. Oh, definitely. With Ma there? No. Oh, that would be weird." And one of them would fall out of the twin bed.

"Very." Jar stripped right down to his briefs before climbing into bed. Jar was all lean muscle and tan skin; he seemed stronger than Scott remembered. Scott admired him as he undressed, then slid in and curled an arm over Jar's waist. He didn't want to push too far, but he didn't want to shy away from anything Jar might be offering either.

Jar tangled their fingers and sighed, relaxing into him.

"Good night, Jar."

"Night, Scotty."

He grinned and dared to kiss Jar's hair. Jar was asleep in seconds.

This wasn't what he'd expected, and it wasn't where he'd expected to be. Nothing was going how he'd thought it would, but it was all right. It was all good.

Everyone he loved was okay.

13

Jarlath blinked his eyes open slowly, knowing even before he moved a muscle that he was going to be sore. He also knew this was going to be a long day, and he wasn't sure if waking up next to Scott was going to make the day easier or harder. It was certainly going to be more complicated.

Scott was asleep on his stomach, and Jarlath let his eyes roam over Scott's smooth, pale skin while he worked up the energy to get out of bed. Last night was the first time he and Scott had ever slept a whole night in bed together, despite all the fooling around they'd done when they were younger. He remembered fantasizing back then about waking up in Scott's arms, wanting what he thought was impossible.

He supposed this didn't count since he hadn't actually woken up in anyone's arms, but he appreciated that Scott had been a gentleman and not asked for more than he'd been able to handle last night.

Jarlath sighed and made himself get up. He was stiff, but not as sore as he'd thought he would be. A long, hot shower should help, some coffee, and he'd be ready to face whatever today threw at him.

He didn't want to. He wanted to crawl back into bed, pull the covers over his head, and pretend he didn't need to call the insurance company or have to tell his people to go on unemployment for a few weeks.

He could hear his dad, though, telling him that when you owned a business, the buck stopped with you. This was his responsibility, and he was going to have to suck it up.

The more tired he was, the longer his shower. He'd always been that way, and so he lingered for a bit, scrubbing and waking up. He toweled off, brushed his teeth, and pulled on a robe. He could smell the coffee before he saw that Scott was out of bed, and he had to grin that they obviously shared that particular addiction.

"Good morning."

"Morning." Scott smiled at him as Jarlath walked into the kitchen. "How did you sleep?"

"I don't know. I was sleeping too hard."

That got him a chuckle. "You were out fast."

"Yeah. I'm sorry I wasn't better company last night." He rubbed his forehead, feeling a little bit of a headache coming on. Already.

"You need to stop apologizing." Scott came to him and took him by the shoulders. "You were exhausted. You still look pretty beat-up."

"I know." He nodded. The sympathy, and the strength in those warm, steady hands, made him uncomfortable and he stepped around Scott, headed for the coffee. "I don't recover as fast as I used to."

"You're not an old man, Jar."

He gave Scott a meaningful look. "Today I feel like one."

"Okay, I hear that. Can I make breakfast?"

Oh, he could totally eat. "You want to? There's eggs and English muffins. I might have some sausage. There's definitely cheese."

"How do you like your eggs?"

"Fried soft. We could make egg sandwiches."

"Oh. Good idea." Scott got to work.

"So...what about you, did you sleep?" He pulled down a mug and poured a cup of coffee.

"I did. But I have chainsaw shoulders this morning."

He knew that ache. "There's Advil in the drawer next to the sink."

"Oh, perfect. Thanks."

He put some milk in his mug and took a breath. "I'm going to put some clothes on. I'll be right back."

"Sure. Of course."

He left the kitchen to find clean jeans and pretended like Scott wandering around his kitchen in a T-shirt and briefs wasn't the sexiest thing he'd seen in a long damn time. He brushed his teeth again and procrastinated a bit, trying to figure out who Scott was to him now. What he wanted.

"Eggs are ready!" Scott called, and he sighed, giving up and going to the kitchen without an answer.

"Smells great." His stomach growled as if on cue.

"Sit." Scott brought two plates over with amazing egg sandwiches on them, and little glasses of grapefruit juice. "I found Pop's juice glasses."

"Every morning. I remember. I haven't used them in...a long time." He'd deliberately changed his routine up after Dad died. Between the house and the pub, he'd felt like he was living with ghosts. And then he'd forgotten about them. Honestly. He understood Scott's nostalgia, though he was reminded that Scott hadn't come home for Dad's funeral.

"I saw the grapefruit juice in the fridge, though."

"Yeah. That rubbed off on me."

Scott picked up his glass. "To Pop O'Connolly," he said and swallowed the juice in one sip. "Yum."

"To Dad." He did the same. "I'm glad he's not here to deal with this."

Scott rolled his eyes. "Eat."

He nodded and took a big bite. "Mmm. Perfect." His mouth was full, so the word didn't come out clearly, but Scott got it and gave him a smile.

"Thank you."

They didn't say anything more as they ate, but every time he glanced up he found Scott studying him. When he was done eating, he got up and dug out a couple of travel mugs. "Coffee to go?"

Scott sighed. "We have to go, huh?"

"No rest for the wicked."

"Speak for yourself." Scott loaded the dishwasher.

"I do. I should be able to get you to Ma's car."

"I'll run home and change, and then I can come back to help. Let me get my jeans on and stuff."

He just nodded. He didn't know what he was going to walk into, and he had no idea how much help he'd need. He knew he had to stop concentrating on Scott, though, and get his head straight. He had real work to do. He filled up their travel mugs, and set them on the counter, before stomping into a pair of sturdy, waterproof work boots.

He put a lantern and another flashlight in his truck, along with the chainsaw, an extension cord, a couple of tarps, and his toolbox. He stored a few things at the pub, but there was no telling what shape they were in.

A few minutes later, they were driving over the bridge that had been closed yesterday. Aside from a broken railing, you'd never know there'd been a huge boat in the middle of the road.

"I'll see you soon," Scott said as he got out of the truck.

"Thanks, man."

Scott closed the door. Jarlath futzed with the radio and his phone and whatever he could until Scott drove off. Ma's car could be temperamental, so he'd stayed to make sure it started. Or that was what he told himself. In reality he was procrastinating, and he knew it.

It was time to go. He straightened up and put his truck in gear.

14

There was still no power when Scott got home. There was a note from Ma telling him to eat the last of the muffins, so he grabbed one and ate half of it on the way to his room. Yes, he'd just had breakfast, so what? *Ma's muffins*. He took a big swig of the coffee Jar had given him and hopped into the shower.

He hated the idea of Jar being over at the pub by himself, and he wasn't going to leave him there long. A quick shower, check in on Ma, and he'd head right over there. He scrubbed and washed, trying to stay focused on the pub, but who was he kidding? Jar had stopped scowling at him and had accepted his help. He'd spent the night in Jar's bed for the first time ever. It didn't matter that it wasn't much more than a snuggle and it was totally chaste; it was more than a just friends thing. A lot more. It certainly meant more to him.

He had a real shot at a second chance here, and he wasn't going to fuck it up again.

He got out of the shower and called Ma while he got

dressed. He was going to have to go without a shave—his electric razor was useless without power.

"Where are you, Scotty?"

"Home. I had a muffin. There's still no power, Ma, so you stay where you are."

"I will. I'm having a marvelous time with the boys. How's Jarlath?"

Hot. As sweet as ever. A champion snuggler. "He's stressed, but he's hanging in there. I'm about to go meet him at the pub. Is it okay if I keep the car?"

"Of course, dear. I'm going to see your father today, but Kate said she would drive me. They didn't lose power, so that was good."

Oh, shit. Dad. "That's good news. Um. Give him a hug for me?"

"Of course. He'll appreciate that, I'm sure."

Maybe. Maybe he'd say he didn't want a hug from a punk. Who knew? "Thanks."

"Oh, hold on son, Jim wants to talk to you."

The phone rattled around a bit before Jim came on the line. "Hey, man. I read that the county hired a contractor to come pick up sandbags. All Jar has to do is call to get on the list. I'll text him the details."

"Oh, great. Thanks."

"And when he's ready for help, call me. I'm available. I don't want to just show up if he's not ready for hands."

"Yeah. I hear that. Thanks, Jim." At the very least, they'd have shutters to take down. But Jim was right, it needed to be done Jar's way and when Jar was ready.

"I'll check in later. Thanks for looking after Ma."

"Oh, it's been great. The kids are entertained, and Kate and I have been able to relax a little. The circumstances aren't the best, but you know, silver linings and all that."

He smiled. "Yep. Enjoy it."

"Talk soon. Here's Ma again."

"You be careful, and give Jarlath our love."

"Will do, Ma. Love you."

"Love you too, son. Bye-bye." Ma hung up.

Scott dug around the garage and found some rubber boots and gloves and a bunch of tools that might be useful, then loaded up the car and got going.

Ezra was setting furniture out in the parking lot when he arrived. He parked well out of the way and grabbed his gloves. "Are they wet?"

"Nope." Ezra grinned at him. "The pallets kept them dry. But the floor is muddy and gross and we need to get everything out."

"Gotcha. Well, I'm here to help."

"Thanks. Nadine is inside directing traffic."

"Traffic?" As soon as the words were out of his mouth, a line of young men came out of the pub wearing masks and carrying dry chairs and tables and some very wet pallets.

"Put the wet stuff in the sun, the dry stuff can stack up over there." Ezra pointed to where he meant.

"Who are these kids?"

"It's the high school football team. School is closed today with no power, so the coach sent them over. Jar is a local sponsor. Well, the pub is. Jar pays for their jerseys and holds fundraisers for new equipment. Stuff like that."

"Wow." *Cool.* "I was Varsity quarterback once. Go Clippers."

Ezra chuckled. "Come on. Jar's in the office, I bet he could use some help. Stay out of the cellar, it's a disaster and is going to need a professional."

"Oh, shit."

"Could be worse, Scott. The water didn't stick around

long." Ezra pulled his mask back up on his face and handed one to Scott as they went inside. "Mostly just smells musty, but you never know."

"Got it." He pulled the mask on.

"See the mud?" They stopped in the pub and scanned the room. The floor was covered for sure and about a foot up the walls. Nadine was setting up mops and buckets while the boys came and went.

"Hey, Nadine." He gave a wave.

"Hey, Scott. Thanks for being here."

He nodded and Ezra led him to the office. "Boss? Scott is here."

"Jar."

"Hi." Jar was sitting on top of Pop O'Connolly's desk, muddy-booted feet hanging over the front. "Thanks, Ezra. Going okay out there?"

"Yeah, the kids are great."

"I'll catch up with you in a bit. I've got a cleanup crew coming later."

Ezra nodded. "We'll get done what we can until they get here. See you in a bit." Ezra gave a wave and left the office.

Jar sighed. "I'm going to have to start over in here."

"I'm sorry." He made his way over slowly, feet squishing in about an inch of muddy gunk.

"Me too. The rug made it, but the furniture is all soaked, and there was some kind of leak..." Jar turned and pointed. "See there, on the far wall?"

There was definitely ruined drywall, and it looked like Jar had poked a hole in the ceiling to let water drain.

"Crap."

"Maybe the roof? Maybe bad gutters, I don't know yet. I have a guy coming out tomorrow."

Damn. Jar was on it. He wondered how long it would be before the pub could reopen.

"Are these masks really necessary?"

"We don't know, so until the cleanup crew gets here and tells us, yes."

"Got it. So what can I do? Ezra thought you might need some help in here."

"I'm trying to figure out where to start. The basement needs pros, the main part of the bar needs some big fans and a good scrubbing....That stuff was easy to get moving. But I just keep looking around in here...at all of Dad's stuff, and I'm just...I can't get moving on it."

He nodded and gave Jar an impulsive hug. Jar stiffened for a second but relaxed quickly and gave him a squeeze back.

"Thanks."

Jar looked kind of frozen, so Scott tried to help with a game plan. "So, how about we take everything you want to keep and put it in your truck?"

Jar nodded slowly. "Okay. That's a good idea; there's no dry place in here for them."

"Okay, good. You want to start with the pictures on the dry walls?"

Jar slid off the desk. "Yeah. That sounds good. And then...maybe the stuff on the desk and the file cabinet?"

"Perfect. Music?"

Jar looked at him. "Music?"

"Well, sure. Why not?"

"Okay. Good idea." Jar pulled out his phone and a second later, there was classic rock coming from a pair of Bluetooth speakers on the desk.

"Rock on. I got this wall."

"This one's mine." Jar picked the long wall near the back

windows and they got to work. Jar's Spotify playlist had finished and gone way off the rails by the time they'd gotten everything that was really important to Jar out of the office. A couple of pictures on the wall close to the leak had gotten pretty wet, but only one picture was in real danger of being ruined, and they decided to take it home to Ma and see if she had some magic up her sleeve.

You never knew with Ma.

They had boxes full of knickknacks and a crate of expensive liquor that had stayed dry, and on their last trip out to the truck, they discovered Nadine had ordered a bunch of six-foot sandwiches from Subway, and the football team was hanging out in the parking lot, stuffing their faces.

"Nadine, great idea. Thank you." Jar set down the box he was carrying and gave her a hug.

"Ooh, I bet I smell." She cringed but she hugged Jar anyway.

"No worse than we do," he offered.

Jar snorted and took his box to the truck. "Speak for yourself, Scotty."

Scotty.

Scott couldn't help his smile. Everything royally sucked right now but somehow, life was pretty good anyway.

He followed Jar and put his box in the truck bed. "One project done. We did pretty good, Jar."

Jar nodded and leaned against the tailgate. "You kicked my butt into gear. Thank you."

"It's not you, you know. This is actually overwhelming."

"I just couldn't get my shit together. I hate to see Dad's office like that."

"It's your office now." He stepped closer, just crossing over the line where things stayed friendly and comfortable. "You can renovate it, make it yours. Pop will still be there, you have pictures, all the important things, but since the desk is toast anyway, why not?"

Jar nodded, looking down at his hands. "It's only been a year."

He knew. He should have been here, but he wasn't. His business had been falling apart, and he was working crazy hours to try to fix it, but that wasn't a reason. It was an excuse. He knew that.

"I'm sorry I wasn't here."

Jar shook his head, and Scott could see his jaw tense, but he didn't say anything.

"I should have been here. For you. For him."

Jar pushed past him and headed back inside, and he followed, not sure what exactly was wrong. Maybe he should have waited to apologize? But how could he let that go? Jar would have thought he was a dick not to at least acknowledge—

"Boss! Cleanup crew is here." Ezra stopped them short just inside the door.

Jar turned around and squinted at Scott, brow furrowed deep, and he had no idea what that meant either. But when Jar turned to Ezra, the cloud just disappeared. "Awesome. Are they down cellar?"

"Yeah. They're having a look and then they're going to—"

"We got some fans in the truck," a voice said from the stairwell on the other side of the cellar door. He heard heavy footsteps on the stairs, then a man appeared in dark coveralls and a Red Sox hat. He had a big grin on his wide face. "Gotta dry it out down there before we can...hey, are you Jarlath?"

Jarlath grinned back and offered a hand to shake. "I am."

"Ah!" The man's voice echoed in the empty pub. "Bill

Kennedy, no relation, but I was a friend of your father's. Good man. Big baseball fan." Scott grinned at the way the man said "*fahthahs.*" Another old salty Cape Codder.

"He was that."

"Remember him well. You have his brow, his chin."

Jarlath nodded. "Mom's eyes."

"This is a heck of a thing, huh? But I've seen worse, I promise you that. We'll get you fixed up. Get some fans going for a couple of days, clean up the mud; then we'll get down there with some Drylok. Don't you worry about a thing."

Jar looked a little green, as if he were torn between relief and throwing up. "Thanks, Bill. I appreciate the positive outlook."

"It's going to take time, kid," Bill said like it was a hard truth. "A week at least. I know that's bad for business, but…"

"Yeah, but I think I was lucky."

Bill winked at Jar and clapped his shoulder. "Atta boy. Keep your chin up. Ezra, you said there was a loading door?"

"Yeah. Back here I'll show you." Bill plodded off with Ezra right behind him.

Jar closed his eyes and sighed. "A week. At least?"

Scott put a hand on Jar's shoulders. "You want to get a beer? Some dinner maybe?"

Jar started to shrug him off but froze for a second and relaxed. "I want a beer. No. I want whiskey."

"Okay. Sure. Whatever you want." He'd drive, let Jar get hammered, whatever Jar needed.

"I need to check on Nadine." But Jar didn't go that way; he took a few steps onto the main floor of the bar.

"Hey, those kids did great." The floor was dirty and still damp, but the goopy mud was all gone. He looked the bar over. The new plywood they'd used to protect it was damp and dirty up to knee height and clean the rest of the way up, marking exactly how high the water had been in here.

"Yeah."

"Your fridges and all that stuff look totally dry."

"Yeah, I seriously lucked out there." Jar nodded. "Just need to air the place out, get the wood all dry, get an electrician in..." Jar sighed again. "Whiskey?"

"Yeah. Come on." Tomorrow. They could deal with that tomorrow. It was getting dark as they left, the last of the kids heading home in their own cars or with parents.

"Hey, Jarlath. I hope you don't mind that I sprung for Subway."

Nadine stopped but Jar walked right up to her and hugged her. "You're amazing. You're...amazing. Thank you."

Nadine smiled and hugged him too, more like a real friend than an employee. That told Scott everything he needed to know about her. "You're not alone, Jar. Okay? Ezra and I already talked about it. One of us will be here every day. Both when we can."

Jar swallowed hard and let her go. "I'll pay you. When the pub opens again, I'll—"

"Jarlath. Stop. We know you will if you can, but we're not worried about it. It's in our best interests to get this place up and running again too. It's your pub, but we love the place."

"Fuck, Nadine." Jar swiped at his eyes. "I'll come back in a few hours to...be here with the fans and all."

"It's all good, Jarlath. Ezra's on tonight because he knows the cleanup guys and wanted to make sure they got set up okay. I've got tomorrow. You're Sunday. Deal?"

Jar nodded. "Deal. Yeah. Thank you."

"Do yourself a favor and get some rest. We've got this. All of us." Nadine gave Jar another quick hug before heading inside. "Night!"

"Night."

He knew Jar had lots of friends, knew the pub was a good place. But he'd had no idea it still ran so much like family. "You've got good people."

"That's an understatement." Jar cut his eyes over, his mouth in a sideways grin. "I'm almost glad you left."

He snorted and shook his head. "Okay, fuck you. I deserve that."

"You promised me a drink."

"So, go get in my car."

"You mean Ma's car? No way. We're taking my truck." Jar pulled out his keys.

"Fine but when you're toasted, I'm driving. No arguments."

The doors chirped as they unlocked. "No arguments. But if you scratch her, we won't be friends anymore."

"And to think I was going to hold your hair while you puked."

Jar laughed. The sound was strange for a second because he hadn't heard it much since he'd been home, and not at all for a couple of days. He took a breath and laughed too as he climbed into Jar's truck.

15

Jarlath knew a little dive out on the highway where he could just be a guy instead of a guy everyone knew with a flooded pub, so that was where he went. He didn't want to talk about the pub, the hurricane, the water, his father, bills...

Actually, he didn't really want to talk at all. He wanted to get a good buzz on, then go home and crash.

Scott must have gotten that vibe, because he turned on the radio and other than singing along, he was quiet the whole way there. Scott still had a good singing voice.

"Oh, man. I forgot about this place," Scott said as Jarlath pulled into the small parking lot.

"It's where I go when I just need a drink, you know?"

Scott nodded. "Sometimes you don't want to know everyone."

He glanced at Scott, then turned off the truck and pulled his keys out of the ignition. "Exactly." He tossed them to Scott, who caught them and gave him a nod.

"Gotcha."

God, it was nice not to have to explain everything.

They went inside and found seats at the bar. Scott ordered him two shots of whiskey and one for himself.

"Thanks. I appreciate you...doing this." He downed one shot immediately and picked up the second.

"What am I doing? You think I don't want a drink?" Scott held up his own and they clinked before swallowing it down.

"Letting me...I don't know. Feel sorry for myself? Wallow? Not feel optimistic?" Decompress. Mourn a little maybe. Just be sad.

"Hey. I'm the guy that skipped prom with you, remember? The guy that didn't give you shit for not coming to my football games."

It was true. Scott never made him feel guilty about anything. "And you came to my drama club stuff anyway."

Scott laughed. "Mhm. And I applauded. Loudly. Louder than Ma, even."

"I remember. It was embarrassing as fuck, but I appreciated it anyway." It was one of the first times he remembered blushing.

"See? I have your back."

He nodded. "You're my guy."

Oh, shit.

He didn't mean that the way it sounded. Or maybe he did, but he wasn't ready to say so and...*fuck fuck fuck.*

Scott looked at him; he could feel those gorgeous eyes on his cheek. "I could be. But don't worry, I'm not in a hurry. You have enough going on right now." Scott didn't sound stressed about what he'd said at all.

He didn't look over; instead he kept his focus glued to the TV. "Thanks." *Thanks? What the hell, Jarlath?* He didn't even know what that meant, so how would Scott? Jarlath tapped the bar and the bartender poured him another shot.

Scott didn't push. "Uh-huh." Scott waved the guy off before he could refill Scott's glass. "I'll just have a Coke, please."

"Driving?"

Scott nodded. "You know it."

"Good man." The bartender filled a glass with Coke and set it down. "Too many guys think it's not cool to be the designated driver."

"I've never been cool, so why start now?" Scott grinned and the bartender grinned.

"I hear that." The bartender tapped the bar and walked away chuckling.

"He likes me. I bet I get this Coke for free."

Jarlath shook his head. "You always were a kiss-ass."

"Me?" Scott looked offended, eyebrows climbing high. "You were the straight-A mama's boy, Jar. Boyish face, so polite, good student..."

"Never crashed a car."

"Shut up."

"Never got caught drinking on the beach." Jarlath winked at Scott.

Scott shook his head. "Caught being the operative word."

It was true. He never got as drunk as Scott did, so he always ran faster. "Never got caught in the back of a car making out with a boy—oh, wait. Yes, I did."

Scott laughed so hard, he almost fell off his barstool. "Jesus, remember that?"

"Mister Logan..."

"*Officer* Logan." Scott put his hands on his hips and

swayed on his stool, sounding like a deep-voiced Kermit the Frog. "Uh...Jarlath. Scotty. You boys had better head home now. It's late."

"And what did you say? 'It's only seven thirty, Officer Logan.' God, I thought you were going to get us in so much trouble."

"But he didn't tell anyone, did he?"

"Not that I ever knew about. And he never said anything to me about it either."

It was a small town. Officer Logan was also Mr. Logan to them, his buddy Sam Logan's father, *and* an assistant varsity football coach. He'd known Scott really well. He could have made a thing about it if he'd wanted to.

But he didn't.

"Me neither. He was a good guy. Crazy, right?"

Jarlath sighed. "I was so into you." *Oh, fuck.* That was the third shot talking. Oh, well. He was just on the verge of not caring.

"We were kids, then. But we're not anymore."

Jarlath shook his head. "No. No, we're not." He looked up to find Scott staring at him, and he remembered that look. That was Scott's "You know you want to blow me" look.

And Scott was right.

"I'm going to—uh. Men's room. Okay? I'll be right back."

"Okay." Scott nodded, watching him.

He went to the men's room and splashed a little cold water on his face. That was it. He was cut off. No more drinking around Scott. He couldn't tell if they were flirting or just airing their regrets. But all of it was awkward.

He dried off and finger-combed his hair before he headed back out to the bar. He wasn't even drunk; he was just tired and not thinking straight. He'd ask Scott to drive him home.

He must have looked confused when he didn't find Scott still sitting at the bar, because the bartender came over. "Your friend settled your bill and said he'd meet you at the truck."

"Oh. Great. Thank you." He tossed a tip on the bar with a sigh. So he was right, it was time to go home. Scott was leaning against the passenger side door when he got outside. "Hey."

"Hey."

"Ready to go, huh?"

Scott nodded and opened the door for him. "Ma got her power back."

"Oh, yeah?"

"I'll pick her up tomorrow and take her home."

"Tomorrow?" He climbed into the truck, blinking as Scott stepped up onto the running board behind him, holding on to the Oh Shit handle for balance.

"I'm busy tonight."

He broke out in goose bumps all over, skin tingling. He was caught in that blue-eyed gaze. "You—"

Scott leaned in and kissed him, a warm hand sliding around to his nape. He was so startled he broke it off for a second, but Scott tugged him in, and this time he didn't hesitate. He returned Scott's kiss, feeling the heat that had been underlying everything for two days grow from long-banked embers to a roaring fire in seconds. That familiar ache that had been with him since the moment he'd caught Scott's eyes grew into something undeniable. He pulled on Scott, wishing they were somewhere else.

Somewhere with a bed.

He broke the kiss off again, panting. "Home. Take me home, Scotty."

"Are you drunk?"

"I'm sober enough to say yes to you and not regret it."

"Yes." Scott nodded and jumped down, closing his door. *Holy fuck. Oh, holy fuck, yes.*

"You sure you're good?" Scott asked as he started up the truck.

"No. I'm burning up. Drive."

"Yeah." Scott leaned over and took another quick kiss.

The ride home made him feel like a teenager again as they stole glances and held hands, grinning at each other like idiots. Jarlath didn't know what else to say, so he let the smiling be enough. Scott looked so handsome driving his truck, a strong profile lit up by the dashboard, and he wanted another kiss, right now.

The water had receded and they drove down Grand Ave, the short and direct route to his house, so it didn't take too long. When Scott put the truck in park, they bailed as if the cab were on fire. Scott grabbed him before he'd made it past the front end and pushed him up against the grill.

"Jar."

"Yeah."

Scott's kiss was different than he remembered. Scott didn't just jam their mouths together, he swept his tongue across Jarlath's lips, so deliberate, tasting him and turning him on. Scott's hands had grown up too and didn't just go right for his fly. They ran up his back and down his arms. They slipped around his waist and pulled their hips together. Hot fingers slid along his jaw.

He moaned, knowing he was being seduced and absolutely on board with it. He hadn't been with anyone like this in a long time. Actually, he wasn't sure he'd been with anyone *like this* ever. Scott felt so good. So right. Fuck, he even smelled good. Jarlath rocked his hips into Scott's and got a groan in answer, and he plunged his fingers into Scott's hair to keep from trying to undress him in the front yard.

"We...should..." Scott leaned back.

He nodded, chasing Scott's lips for more kisses, drunk on Scott now more than the whiskey. "Uh-huh."

"Keys."

"You have them?" He tucked a hand into Scott's pocket and followed Scott's lead into his dark house.

He locked the door as Scott tossed his keys onto the hall table, and then everything went wild. Their kiss was sloppy and urgent as they undressed each other on the way to his bedroom. Scott had a strong, musky scent that had Jarlath breathing deep, and he wasn't built like a kid anymore. He had full muscles and broad shoulders and arms that Jarlath wanted around him.

Jarlath kicked off his shoes and tossed his jeans and briefs as they neared the bed, and Scott put a hand on his chest to stop him. He was so surprised, he whimpered. "Scott."

"Wait. Jar. I want to look at you."

His face flushed and he was glad for the near darkness, but the room was lit by moonlight, so Scott could see everything else.

"You're beautiful. I don't remember you so..."

"Grown up?"

"Yeah, I guess." Scott smiled. "Yeah."

"I was thinking the same about you. We're different now in a lot of ways."

"We are. We're not kids, and I'm not going to treat you like one, Jar. I want to hold you. I want to have you."

Jar nodded a stepped forward. "I've missed you."

Scott pulled him in. "I'm sorry."

He put a finger over Scott's lips. "Don't tell me. Show me."

That got him another sweet smile with a look that quickly grew heated. "I'd like that."

He climbed back onto the bed and Scott slid over him to kiss him again. Jarlath reached between them and brushed his hand over a hard nipple on his way lower, over Scott's navel and even lower, into his curls. Scott panted in his ear and rocked his hips, pushing a hungry cock into his hand with a soft hiss.

"For me?" he teased, and pet it gently, fingers running over hot skin. He wrapped his hand around Scott's shaft and tugged a little, and Scott groaned and dropped his head to Jarlath's shoulder.

Scott let him touch a little, but not as long as he'd wanted to. A second later Scott was sliding down his body, dropping kisses along the way, leaving a trail that started hot, then cooled enough to make him shiver.

"Scott."

"Got a promise to keep, baby."

Scott cradled his balls and rolled them, touched his tongue to the tip of Jarlath's prick, and made Jarlath gasp, hands going back into Scott's hair. "Yes."

"I've got you, Jar. I'm going to be so good to you." Scott tasted with his tongue and stroked with his fingers before closing his lips over the head of Jarlath's cock.

"Oh. God."

"Mm." Scott hummed and took him deeper, making him ache from his thighs to his ribs. He followed what Scott was doing to him at first—tracked the movement of that hot tongue, felt each round of suction and friction—but he lost the thread after a bit and just floated on a wave of pure need.

"So good. Fuck. Yes." He babbled and praised and took shallow and shuddering breaths until Scott eased up, leaving him wanting. "Oh. Oh, God. Don't stop. Scott—"

"Rubbers, baby. Condoms. Where?"

Jarlath whimpered as he stretched an arm out to open a drawer in his nightstand.

Scott dove for it. "Got it. Got it, baby. Hang on."

He watched as Scott rolled it on, loving the tiny little grimace. "Lube is—"

"Yup. On it. Fuck, I want you." Scott was breathing hard and kept biting his lips.

The lube was cool against his hole, and he hauled one knee up to give Scott more access. He was ramped up. Aching. "Want you. Please."

Scott pushed a finger inside him and he gasped again. That was good, that was something, but it wasn't enough. Thankfully, Scott stretched and teased him just right and didn't make him wait long. Those fingers disappeared, replaced immediately with the sweet pressure of Scott's prick.

"Yes. It's good. Yes, Scott." He nodded and pulled his knees higher.

They hadn't fucked but a few times, and they'd never done it face-to-face before. He watched Scott's expression, taking in the furrow of that strong brow and the way Scott's lips formed an almost perfect O.

"Beautiful. God. So beautiful." Scott tossed his head and sank in deep, making Jarlath shout.

"Fuck!" Jesus, that was perfect. "More."

Scott's groan was heavy and deep. "Jar...fuck, you feel so good."

He planted his feet on the bed and rocked up, letting Scott know in no uncertain terms what he wanted.

"Mother of—" Scott grunted and began to move, long strokes that took him deep and hard. He hooked his heels behind Scott's ass and rocked up to meet them. The room filled with the sounds of their panting and grunting as they moved together. He kept one hand in Scott's hair and the other curled around Scott's shoulder, holding on tight.

He'd been thinking about this, wanting it but not wanting to say so, since those blue eyes walked into his pub again.

"Jar...Jar." Scott's panting grew shallow, and he took Jarlath's prick in hand, jacking him steadily and bringing him to the edge of his orgasm.

"Scott! Yes. I...I'm gonna..." Oh, fuck was he ever. He trembled, and his climax shot through him like lightning. He gasped, feeling as though he might shake to bits as he soaked Scott's fingers and belly, his own scent rising between them.

And Scott was right behind him.

"Yes. Fuck. Jar!" Scott shouted and his hips stuttered as he arched and shot, swelling and pumping inside Jarlath and making him moan.

They clung to each other, harsh breaths and groans fading into sweet, slow kisses and gentle sounds. Scott ditched the rubber and settled in beside him, pulling him into those strong arms.

"Wow." He sighed and tucked his head under Scott's chin.

"Wow," Scott agreed, nodding. "You're...you...Jesus, Jar."

Yeah. Yes, exactly. "You showed me, huh?"

"I hope so."

Jarlath looped an arm over Scott's waist and snuggled in closer. He was going to close his eyes and sleep—really sleep—for the first time in a few nights. He promised himself that he wouldn't question this in the morning, and whatever else happened between them, he knew he wouldn't regret this. He'd needed it. *They* had.

He felt Scott sigh and settle with him, and everything was good for now. He was going to have some sweet dreams.

16

Scott woke up with a smile. He had his arms around Jar, it was a beautiful sunny morning, and they'd just fu —*no*. No, they'd made love for the first time ever. He was lying here with his best friend and the only man he'd ever really fallen for, the man he'd missed but didn't know how to say so because he'd been the one who left town. He had never dreamed he'd deserve this if he was going to be that far away, and it would never have been fair to Jar.

Then come to find out Jar didn't want anyone else either. How crazy was this? He'd left California at loose ends, not sure what he was going to do with himself next, not sure if he was going to go back or not, not even sure whether he wanted to. But he'd finally managed to do something right, and now everything was clear. He was staying, he was going to be with Jar, and he was only moving forward. He wasn't going to worry about the past; he was going to hold on to Jar and find a future.

"You're thinking loudly," Jar mumbled against his chest.

He chuckled. "How did you even know I was awake?"

"The way you breathe. And you sighed."

"I sighed?"

"Mhm." Jar turned his head up and kissed his chin. "Morning."

Scott shared his smile with Jar and kissed his forehead. "Good morning."

"How did you sleep?"

Like the dead. "So well. I crashed hard. That was a hell of a day."

"Mhm. It was a tough one, but it ended well." Jar was still waking up and sounded so sweet and sleepy.

"Yes. I couldn't have asked for a better ending to the day."

Jar yawned, rolled onto his back, and stretched long, and Scott got to admire all the lean, tan muscle. "Are you going to make me breakfast again?"

"I can do that." Food would be good for Jar.

"I have so much to do today. I'm dreading it."

"I know. And I have to go pick up Ma and get her settled at home; then I told her we'd go see Dad. He's not real good on the phone."

"Yeah, I know. I tried to call when he was first—when Ma first agreed to let him go there, and it was awful. I don't anymore, I just go to see him once a week."

"That's nice of you."

Jar shrugged. "Well, he's the dad I have left, you know?"

Scott nodded. His parents had been like Jar's forever. "He's not doing great, is he?"

Jar sighed. "No. He's not. I mean, he has good days. But his bad days are really bad. He gets combative and angry, I think he just gets scared when he can't remember what's going on. They sometimes give him meds to keep him calm, but then it's like visiting with a zombie. They haven't found the right answer yet."

"He definitely has crystal-clear moments, Jar. The last time I took Ma, he stared me down and told me he needed me to stay in town and take care of her. He made me promise."

Jar nodded. "He's happy you're here. He's missed you."

Scott sighed. He wanted to believe that. "I need to see as much of him as I can now, I guess."

"So that's why you decided to stay?" Jar reached out and combed fingers through his hair. "Dad?"

He looked into Jar's dark eyes. They were so brown it was hard to see the pupils, even in the brightly lit room. "That's what decided it. But when he and I had that talk, I was already hoping I'd have another reason."

"Stuffed quahogs?" Jar grinned at him.

"Oh. Yes, definitely. The spicy ones."

"I'm glad you're staying. I'm glad we're getting...this. To try this. You know?"

"I know." He leaned forward and took a kiss, hooking his fingers behind Jar's head. Jar opened for him, let him have the kiss and then some. He kept hold of Jar as their lips parted.

Jar blinked at him a little stupidly, and it was adorable.

"I wasn't sure San Francisco was where I belonged anymore, anyway."

"I wondered. Ma said things went south with your company."

He blinked, surprised that Ma knew that, and even more surprised that she'd told Jar. "It's...uh, yeah. It was good while it lasted." It wasn't good now; it was finished. He'd saved a little money, but it wasn't going to last him very long.

"Sorry about that. I know it was what you wanted."

"Thanks. It really was."

Jar gave him a curious look. "And now?"

"Now, all I want is you." But he knew this couldn't only be about what he wanted. "I—"

"Scott? Can I just get something off my chest?"

Like he was just about to do? So weird how in tune they were, even after all that time apart. "Yeah. Of course."

"I've spent a lot of time being angry with you, and I really want to let it go, but part of me just isn't...totally over it yet."

Well, fuck. But Jar was holding his hand tight, so how awful could this be? "Okay...I mean, I don't expect you to just brush it all off. I know I have a lot to make up to you."

"I don't know. It's not really like that. I just need you to know that not calling me and not coming to Dad's funeral...I was very hurt, and I don't want to get hurt again. I told myself I wouldn't let it be an issue, but..." Jar rolled his eyes. "Here we are. So."

"I get it. This is on me. I blew it in a big way, and I own that. But I'm trying. Okay? I am." He planned to earn Jar's trust any way Jar would let him. "No expectations, no taking you for granted. I promise."

That was what he'd wanted to say before.

Jar nodded and puffed out a breath. "Thank you. I just want to start new, you know?"

Oh, he was all for that. He leaned in to get another one of Jar's kisses.

And Jar's phone rang.

"Oh, boy."

Jar groaned and rolled over to grab it. "It's Ma," he said before answering. "Hey, Ma....Yes, he's here."

"In my bed..." Scott whispered, playing.

Jar put a finger to his lips, but he was grinning. "Yes, he's going to come get you....Your car is fine....We're just having breakfast."

"Liar," he whispered.

Jar poked him hard.

"Ow!"

"What?...Oh, Scott just stubbed his toe. We'll finish up and he'll be on his way. He can tell you all about the pub. We had the football team helping, did you hear?"

Scott waggled his eyebrows. "Why do you have a dildo in your nightstand?"

"What?" Jar stared at him and drew a line across his neck with one finger. "Sorry. Yes, he knows you want to go see Dad....He's good....Thanks, Ma. Love you too. Bye."

"It's a legit question."

"You're in so much trouble."

He laughed, hauling himself up to sitting. "You're blushing."

"It's a vibrator, if you must know, and I'm not blushing. That was Ma! She doesn't need to know these things."

"You think Ma never had a vibrator?"

"Oh, my God." Jar covered his ears and got out of bed. "La la la la, I am not listening."

Scott chased Jar into the shower. But as much as they both wanted to fool around, they didn't really, beyond a few touches and kisses. Ma needed him, and Jar had work to do. They'd have time later.

After their shower, they danced around each other in the kitchen, making coffee and breakfast wraps.

"Did you cook a lot in San Francisco?" Jar asked, adding a little cream to his cup.

"Yeah, actually. I like to cook, and I'm pretty good at it. At the very least, I can follow a recipe." He'd lived alone, and when he wasn't working he'd had time on his hands.

"Cool. I usually eat at the pub just because I'm there, but I like to grill at home. I make a lot of fish."

"We should grill one night soon. Sit out on the dock like we used to with Pop." They used to spend a lot of time fishing or crabbing in the pond, and they'd cook it for dinner. It was a fond memory.

"I miss that. We did it a couple of nights a week right up until he died."

Scott sighed. "I should have been here for you."

"Don't...we've been over that. I mean, maybe so? I was really upset at the time, but Ma kept reminding me that Pop didn't want a big thing anyway."

"He had a big thing, though. Kate told me all about it." Jar had taken the *Jenny* out alone to scatter Pop's ashes in Vineyard Sound and when he got back, half the town had gathered at the pub for a memorial.

Jar nodded. "I didn't plan that."

"No, but you can't stop people from caring about him if they want to." He rubbed Jar's shoulder. "Or you."

Jar chuckled. "There are a lot of good people in this town."

Scott put a wrap in front of Jar. "Chow down. Then we'll get going. Ma will be calling me next to see where I am."

"She did sound a little anxious. She loves the boys, but she gets tired. I think at home she can go to her room and have a nap and not feel like she's letting anyone down."

Scott nodded. That sounded about right. He took a bite of his wrap. "Mmm. Good."

"I'm so spoiled. Normally, I'd have a bowl of cereal or pick something up at Dunkin' Donuts on the way in."

"Doughnuts have their place, I love a good jelly doughnut. But life is too stressful for sugary breakfast. You need some stick-to-your-ribs food."

"You really are your mother's son."

Scott hoped so. Mostly. She was a kind, wise, loving woman. He'd be happy to take after her.

They finished eating, cleaned up, got out of the house before anyone called him, and made the short drive to the pub. It was a gorgeous day; if not for the muddy road and the debris-covered beach, you wouldn't have known there'd been a hellish storm barely two days ago.

"Thanks for everything, Scott," Jar said as they climbed out of the truck. "You've been—"

"It was my pleasure," he interrupted.

"I was going to say a pain in the ass." Jar grinned and tangled their fingers, walking him to the sedan.

"Shut up." He leaned over and kissed Jar's cheek.

"Seriously. Thank you for your help yesterday and...and last night was amazing. I want more. I want to see you later. Tonight."

That made Scott's chest ache in the best way. "Maybe come for dinner? I know Ma will want to see you. Make sure you're okay."

"Yeah. Cool. Let me know when."

"I'll call you." He took a quick kiss and climbed into Ma's car. Jar gave him a wave and took a step back, then turned and headed for the pub.

Scott turned on the radio and sang along, feeling...great. Jar wanted more. It was good to be wanted, it was...it made him happy. Proud. He was doing it right this time.

17

"Hello?"

"Hey, Jarlath, it's Kate."

He knew that, he had caller ID. But Kate always said it anyway. "Hey, Kate. How did you and Jim make out? Scott said you kept power, huh?"

"Yeah. We lucked out. Good thing because Ma—well, you know she lost power. Scott picked her up a little while ago."

"Everything okay?"

"Yes. I was calling to ask you the same question. I'm sorry I haven't been down there yet."

"No worries, you looked after Ma. That's important."

"How is the place?"

Jarlath took a breath and wandered outside. He'd always been honest with Kate; she was like a big sister. She was his confidant, his sounding board. "It's...I keep telling myself that I was lucky mostly, but it's still kind of a mess."

"Is it going to be a tough cleanup?"

"I don't know. It's going to need time, water doesn't just

disappear, you know? They have to dry it out. But Ezra found a great company—the guy who owns it knew Dad, so...it's good. I trust him. They're going to start scrubbing and dealing with the main floor while the basement dries out, which will take a lot more work."

"Wow. Did they say how long?"

"A week at least, so I'm thinking two, maybe?" A long time. Usually he came off a summer tourist season in good shape. But this season had ended a week or so early, and the profit he'd made would all go toward restocking and reopening. It could be a tough winter while he waited for his insurance money to come through.

"At least—well, that's a long time, but it could be worse, right?"

She meant well with that comment, he knew that, but it still made him cringe. "Yeah, it could be. I still have the place."

"Are you okay?" Kate sounded genuinely concerned; she wasn't just being nice.

"I'm...yeah. I think?" He'd have been much worse if he hadn't unloaded on Scott. Scott had a good ear.

And good hands. And a really nice—

"So what's next?"

"Hm? Next?" He blinked.

"At the pub."

"Oh. Right, sorry." *Wow*. He'd gotten a little distracted. "Nadine and I are cleaning Dad's office. We tore up the carpet and washed the floor. It's hard, though. We lost so much of his stuff. His big oak desk is toast."

"Oh, I'm sorry, Jarlath. I know there's a lot of history there."

"There is. But we managed to save a lot of stuff. Scott was a big help going through some of it yesterday."

"Right. He said you guys did a lot of work. He looked a little wiped out, you know? Like he hadn't gotten enough sleep..." Kate's tone was suggestive.

Jarlath huffed a soft laugh. She was pretty perceptive when she wanted to be. "Yeah. He didn't sleep all that well last night."

"I'm sorry to hear that. Nightmares?" She was teasing him now. Maybe Scott had said something.

"You're funny."

"So, I'm right? Are you guys a thing again?"

Were they a thing again? He wasn't sure. "I...I don't know that I'd call us a *thing*."

"I knew it! I knew it! God, I'm so glad he's home." He thought he heard her clapping with glee.

"Listen, Kate. Don't make a big thing out of this yet, okay? I'm not sure exactly where we stand right now, and I don't want to...screw it up, you know?" They were a little beyond trying to take it slow, but he still felt like they needed to work some things out. "Like, don't say anything to Ma yet, okay?"

"Oh. Oh, yeah, I get it. No worries, Jarlath. I'm just really happy for you both."

"Thanks." Of course, Ma had a way of knowing things, and she knew Scott better than anyone, so it might not stay a secret for long. "I'm going over there for dinner tonight."

"You're going for dinner, and you think Ma's not going to figure out what's going on between you and Scott?"

Kate had a good point. "Yeah, I hear what you're saying." He sighed. "I just...Kate, honestly, I don't want people to find out we're seeing each other again and make some big deal of it and then...and then have it fall apart and disappoint everyone." Again.

"Oh, Jar. I just want you to be happy."

"I know. I know." He nodded as if she could see him. He'd like to be happy too. He was once. And Scott had definitely made him happy last night. He just didn't totally trust it yet. "I appreciate that. I do."

"We're all going to kick his ass if he breaks your heart again, Jarlath. You know that, right?"

Jarlath laughed. "Well, I guess I don't have anything to worry about then, do I?"

"Hey, Boss?" Nadine stuck her head out the door. "The crew has a question for you. You got a minute?"

"Yeah. Yes. Hang on." He waved to Nadine and she went back inside. "Hey, Kate? I gotta run."

"Of course. Be careful and try to take a break once in a while, okay? I worry about you a little."

"Just a little?" Kate worried about him like he was one of her sons.

"Shut up, it's my job as your chosen big sister."

"You're the best, Kate. Love you."

"Love you, Jarlath. Talk soon, okay?"

"You got it. Thanks." He hung up the phone.

When he got inside, the main part of the bar was all lit up. At first he thought they'd gotten power back but then he remembered everything was shut off at the main until they could get the place inspected. These were the team's battery-operated floodlights. "Bright in here."

"Jarlath!" Bill Kennedy marched over to him, smiling. "Your basement is good. Everything is cleaned up and the fans are running off our generator out in the parking lot. We'll keep the genny gassed up while we work in here. I'd still say give it a week, then we'll do that Drylok coat, and you'll be good down there."

He nodded. A week was what Bill had said to expect.

"But up here, we can get you going in three or four days I'd think."

"Yeah?" That was a pleasant surprise. "You think?" If he could get the inspector out before Friday, maybe he could open with a reduced capacity for the weekend. The summer crowd was gone, so they wouldn't fill up anyway.

Bill nodded, sure of himself. "I've done a lot of these, kid."

"That's great." He made his way over to the bar. "You took the fridges down, huh? Where did you stash them?"

"In the walk-ins for now. They stayed dry."

"Oh, good idea."

"Yeah, and the box you built to keep them all high and dry didn't keep the bar dry, but it did keep it from getting dinged or scratched by debris. Let it dry another day, then strip the sides and refinish them, and you should be good."

"Cool." Tomorrow's project. "And the floor?"

"I think we can save it. It might end up a bit faded-looking, though. With the off-season coming you could probably refinish it in stages, you know? One area at a time so you can stay open."

"Yeah. Yeah, good idea." He took a deep breath and puffed it out. It was a lot, but it was getting handled. This wasn't a disaster, right?

Bill clapped him on the shoulder. "You're all right, kid. I promise I've seen so much worse. I've saved worse. This is all going to be okay."

He nodded slowly. "Thanks." He turned to look at Bill. "Really, thank you. It's—I can't tell you what it means to know I can just trust you with this."

Bill gave him a smile. "It's never good news when someone has to call me in. Never. I try to make a bad thing feel...well, maybe not better, but less overwhelming, you know?"

"It feels like you took a big weight off my shoulders, Bill. Let me know if your team needs anything, okay?"

"You got it."

There was a crash in the office, and Nadine swore loudly. He and Bill looked at each other.

"Go on, kid. I've got work to do."

"Yep. Thanks." He took off at a jog. "Nadine?"

"I'm fine. I'm fine, Boss. Sorry. Just stupid." Nadine snarled the last word and limped across the office.

"You okay? What happened?"

"I was taking the drawers out of the file cabinet and I dropped that one on my fucking toe." Nadine took another step. "Ow."

He and Scott had emptied the drawers into boxes and everything was at the house, but the cabinet was so waterlogged it had to go out to the dumpster.

"Jesus, Nadine. Sit down, I'll get you some—uh." He rolled his eyes. "No ice. I'll find you an ice pack."

"I'm fine. I just need to walk it out. Sorry."

"You're tired. You should go home and get some rest."

"I'm waiting on Ezra to come in."

"I'm here. I can wait for Ezra." It was his damn job after all.

"I am fine." Nadine leveled him with a look, but it was softened by the little smile tugging at one corner of her lips. "You're on tomorrow, and I can sleep all day. Let's get this done so you can get to fixing it up again."

"All right, but take it easy on that foot."

There was a knock at the open office door, and he and Nadine both turned to see who was there.

"Hey, Boss."

"Benny!" Nadine limped over and gave Benny a hug. "How are you? How's Celia and baby Michael?"

"We're good. We're all good. Exhausted. Michael is a handful and a half." Benny hugged her back. "Wow, look at this mess."

Jarlath sighed. "I know. But we're trying to look on the bright side."

"Sure. Of course," Benny agreed easily. "What can I do?"

"Do? You've got a brand-new baby, Benny. You don't need to be here."

"Oh. Yeah. Yes. Yes, I do." Benny nodded. "I need to not be home for a couple of hours."

Nadine laughed. "Oh, boy."

"Celia's mom is there. You know, they don't need me hanging around."

Jarlath tried to get it. He didn't really understand kids and mothers-in-law, but he understood that Benny needed something else to do. "Well, listen. I was just trying to get Nadine to take a load off. She hurt her foot. So how about you help me in here so Nadine can go home?"

"Is that what the limp is about? Hell yeah, Nadine. Go home."

"I sense a conspiracy." Nadine looked at Benny. "Are you sure you can stay for a while? I was going to hang out until Ezra came in."

"Yeah. Totally. Nobody is going to miss me for a few hours."

Nadine looked between them. "Okay. Okay, Boss, you win. I'll see you uh...Monday, I guess."

"Monday. Thanks, Nadine. Get some sleep, and let me know if you need anything for that foot, okay?" She was an employee, but she was also a friend.

"Thanks. Later, guys."

Benny watched her go. "I'm sorry I haven't been around more, Jar."

Jarlath waved him off. "You're joking, right? We had a hurricane two days after your Michael was born. You've been a little busy. But I appreciate that you're here, your timing was good. Nadine's been working hard."

"So, what needs doing?"

"Okay. Cool. The file cabinet, those chairs, pretty much everything you're looking at needs to go out to the dumpsters."

"Heavy lifting. Can do."

Benny was a big guy; "can do" was an understatement. He picked up the empty file cabinet and took it out by himself. Jarlath followed with one of his father's armchairs. He tried to just work and not think too hard about losing all of Dad's stuff, and Benny made that easy because he was doing the same thing. They had the office empty in under an hour. It was just a bare room now—a room badly in need of cleaning, a new carpet, and a paint job.

He'd start on that tomorrow.

"So, Jarlath," Benny said coming back to the office with two bottles of water. He handed one to Jarlath. "I'm sure this place is going to be closed for a bit, but Celia is going to need me at home for a few weeks."

"Sure. Paternity leave like we'd planned?"

"I guess so. Her mom is going to have some chemo...and—"

"Oh, man. I hope your mother-in-law recovers quickly. You think you'll need more time than we talked about?" He understood, and Benny deserved the time with his family, but he was going to be short a bartender. He and Ezra could probably figure it out.

"I don't know yet. But Celia can't take care of the baby and her mom at the same time, you know?"

"I know. You get to be a good dad. That's awesome."

"I'm really sorry."

"Don't be. Family first, Benny. And it's the off-season, we'll be okay." It actually might save him a little money to bartend himself and if he had to, he could hire some temp—

Some temporary help...

Gosh, wherever would he find an unemployed bartender?

"We'll be totally fine."

Benny nodded. "Us too, I hope."

"I'm so sorry about your mother-in-law. Is Celia okay?"

"I think so. It's a little scary. But the doctors are hopeful, so we are too." Benny sucked down his water in two gulps.

"Good. That's good, Benny."

"Excuse me." Benny pulled a ringing cell phone out of his pocket. "Hey, sweetheart....Oh, good idea....Sure, I'll pick something up on the way home."

He gave Benny a thumbs-up and mouthed, *Go ahead.*

Benny nodded and shook Jar's hand. "Yeah, I'm just leaving now, in fact..."

Jarlath gave Benny a wave, and Benny made the universal sign for "I'll call you" and left.

He went back out to the main room, got another bottle of water, and watched the cleanup crew for a bit. There was so much work to do, and he still needed to sit down and figure out what his inventory losses actually were. All the food, the beer, the liquor, the furniture...what he was losing each day he was closed, plus refinishing the bar and the floors and redoing the office and—

And he had to pass inspection just to get the lights turned on.

He needed some help. He needed some food. He needed a blowjob.

He needed Scott.

Jarlath finished his water and texted Ezra to find out when he'd be in.

18

Scott chuckled as Jarlath leaned back in his chair with a groan. "Thank you. Dinner was so good, Ma."

He understood. He was absolutely stuffed.

Ma smiled and laid a hand on Scott's arm. "Oh, you should thank Scotty, he did the grilling."

"Ma, those roasted potatoes and veggies were amazing." He lifted his arm and kissed his mother's hand.

"Too kind, both of you." Ma pushed her chair away from the table and stood.

"Oh." Jar hopped up. "You sit, Ma. I'll do the dishes. Let me take your plate." Jar's hand ghosted over Scott's shoulders as he walked by, such a small gesture, but it gave Scott the shivers all the same, the little hairs on the back of his neck standing up.

Jar scooped up all three plates like the professional pub owner he was and carried them into the kitchen.

"Jarlath is such a darling boy. Always has been. So sweet." Ma set her napkin on the table and picked up her water glass.

"Mm. That was subtle, Ma."

Ma pretended to look horrified. "It was just an observation, Scotty."

He nodded. She was observant, for sure. He grinned at her. "Any other observations you'd like to share?"

"Well." Ma put her glass down and leaned closer. "Just that if you're still interested in him, Jim and Kate think now would be a good time to—you know—since he needs so much help."

Kate and Jim. He should have known they'd talk about him behind his back, especially knowing he was staying the night at Jar's place. Twice. "To...*you know*?" He crossed his arms over his chest. "Whatever do you mean, Ma?"

"Oh, Scotty. He's such a nice boy."

"Man. He's a man now, Ma. We're both grown men." Ma blushed, and he winked at her.

"Well, of course I know that." She tried to look offended. "Really, Scotty."

He knew he should stop torturing her, but it was too much fun. "You think I should ask him out?"

Ma smiled. "Well, that might be a nice thing to do."

"Oh, wait. Too late, I already did, and he said yes. We went out last night."

Ma's eyes grew wide and she clapped her hands together. "Oh, Scotty! I'm so glad to hear it."

"Is it safe for me to come back yet?" Jar called from the kitchen.

"I think so. What do you think, Ma?"

"Oh, for the love of Pete." Ma made a face and shook her head. "Honestly, you boys are too much."

He had to laugh. "I knew we couldn't keep it from you; you know us both too well."

"Well, it's true. I do know my boys."

"Ma." Jarlath sat down again. "This is new still, and we both want to keep it quiet for a bit yet, okay?"

Had they said that? They wanted to keep it quiet? Scott didn't want to keep it quiet; he wanted to show Jar off, let everyone know he was back now, and he wasn't going to screw it up this time.

But Jar had spoken for the both of them, and if that was what Jar wanted, he couldn't very well disagree, could he?

"Well, that's just fine. But I know just how this will turn out." Ma looked so pleased with herself.

Jar snorted. "You do, huh? Well, you keep that to yourself and tell me I told you so later. Okay?"

Ma nodded. "You boys take all the time you need. Just let me know."

"Let me know" probably meant Ma wanted to throw a party or something. She was already planning it in her head; he was sure of it.

"How about dessert?" Jar had stopped in town and picked up *pastéis de nata* from the Portuguese bakery. The little custard tarts were Ma's favorite.

"I saved room!" Ma looked pleased. "I have blackberries in the refrigerator."

Scott got up. "I've got this. You two sit."

He could hear them chatting as he took out the berries and started some coffee. Jar was telling Ma about sandbags and the football team, and about the giant fans they'd set up to dry things out.

"Opening in a week, you think?"

"Drying out in a week. Opening...I don't know. I have to get an inspector in and get a green light, and then we have to restock and get everyone back on the schedule..." Jar sighed.

Scott brought the pastries out and set them down on the

table. "Ma. Give Jar a break. He's been mired in this for days."

"Oh. Oh, you're so right, Scotty. I'm sorry, Jarlath. I'm just curious and I—"

"It's fine, Ma. I'm fine. I'm a little tired, and I don't have all the answers yet is all." Jar sounded more than a little tired to him.

"Well, of course you don't." Ma took Jar's hand. "You call me Ma like Kate and Scotty do for a reason. It's because you are family, and we love you. Anything one of us would do for each other, we would do for you too. You remember that. You call on your family when you need us."

Jar nodded and Scott saw him swallow hard before speaking. "Thank you, Ma. I love you too." Jar looked at his hand in Ma's for a long moment, studying their fingers, then took a big breath and looked up at Scott. "Do I smell coffee?"

Oh. That was his cue. "Yes. Let me get some mugs."

"Don't these look delicious?" He heard Ma ask as he headed back into the kitchen. He returned with coffee for him and Jar and a cup of hot water and a tea bag for Ma. "These are so good, Scotty. Sit and try one."

"They are pretty damn—*darn*—good. Sorry, Ma." Jar took a big bite and did seem to be enjoying it.

He cut into his with his fork and took a bite. The creamy custard was smooth and not too sweet. He'd been eating these since he was a kid from that same bakery, and he knew them well. He forked up a couple of blackberries to go with it. "Delicious." Maybe tomorrow he'd grab Ma some sweet bread.

Jar drank down his coffee and had a second cup before pushing away from the table. "I am so full."

"Me too," Ma agreed. "I was just thinking I would turn in. You boys don't mind the dishes?"

"No, we've got it. Thank you again for dinner." Jar hopped up and pulled out her chair.

"You've had a tough week, I was glad I could feed you."

He offered Ma his arm. "I'm just going to help Ma get settled, Jar. I'll be back in a minute."

"Sure. See you in the kitchen." Jar got up and disappeared.

"You don't have to fuss over me."

"You're right. I don't have to." He winked at Ma and let her lean on him a little on the way to her bedroom. She seemed tired.

"Silly boy. I do appreciate it, though. My grandsons wear me out. Hopefully by tomorrow I'll be more myself."

"I'm sure you will be." It didn't take him long to make sure she had what she needed. He kissed her good night and closed her door on the way out, only then realizing he hadn't asked whether Jar could spend the night. Not that it would be a very comfortable sleepover.

Jar had most of the kitchen cleaned up by the time he was done with Ma, and the dishwasher was already running.

"Hey." He stepped up next to Jar and leaned a little.

Jar leaned right back. "Hey. She's all settled?"

"Yeah. She's exhausted. I think she's happy about it, though."

"It's all the family time, and you being home. All is right in her world." Jar smiled at him and tossed him a dishtowel. "Dry the pots?"

"On it." Jar finished washing the last couple of pots and he dried them; then they both looked around the kitchen carefully.

"Did we forget anything?"

"I don't think so." Jar chuckled. "I don't want her to come in here in the morning and roll her eyes at us, you know?"

"I think we're good. I'll wipe down the dining room table."

"Cool." Jar watched him, hanging out in the kitchen doorway. "So...I guess I should go?"

He sighed. *Dammit.* "I wanted to ask her if you could stay, but I forgot."

"Oh. No. That's okay. We can...uh." Jar rubbed the back of his neck. "I'll see you tomorrow, I guess."

"You want to go for a ride?"

"A ride?"

"Sure. On my bike?" It was a little dark but...

Jar's head tilted. "Or you could just come home with me."

Scott nodded. "I didn't ask Ma about that either."

"So, leave her a note?" Jar suggested.

Was he a fool? Jar had just asked him to go home with him. Twice. "Yes. I'll leave a note."

"Her desk. Top drawer."

Scott grinned at Jar. "Had this all planned out, did you?"

"Maybe. Maybe I've been thinking about you all night."

Oh, he liked the heated tone in Jar's voice. "Dear Ma. I've gone to Jar's place. I have my phone," he said out loud as he wrote the note. "Call me if you need anything." He set the paper down on the kitchen table, then looked at Jar. "Let me pack a bag. I want to help at the pub tomorrow; I can just ride over with you."

"I can bring you home first, it's no big deal."

He looked at Jar. "Stay right there." He was going to pack a bag, and they'd talk about this whole down-low situation tomorrow. He packed enough for a couple of days because if this was going in the sleepover direction, he was going to want to keep a few things at Jar's place. When he came back, Jar had turned all the lights out and was waiting for him in the foyer.

"Ready?"

"Yes." He caught Jar's arm, pulled him close, and kissed him. Jar didn't hesitate to move in closer and return the kiss.

"Let's go." Jar tugged on him. "I want you."

Yeah, he knew how that was. Jar's kisses made him feel like the horny teenager he used to be.

Maybe he could handle the down-low if it meant he would have this.

19

Jarlath had been through some long weeks in the past. The week Scott left town. The week his father died. The week he and Jim spent convincing Ma that she couldn't care for Ned at home anymore. The week following Hurricane Eric had been hard too.

It probably wasn't the very worst week of his life, but it seemed like the longest. His list of things he needed to do now that the place was finally dried out was so long, he didn't know where to start. Figuring that out was the next thing on his agenda—as soon as the inspector was finished going over the building.

He was nervous. He thought things looked pretty good, but what did he know? This could go well, or it could go horribly sideways.

God, his stomach hurt.

He tried to focus on the good things. The roof was sound. The windows were intact. The electrical box was on the main floor behind the bar and had stayed well above the water line, so he was definitely lucky there too. The basement had been totally underwater, but all the wiring was in the ceiling so even if that had to be replaced it wouldn't be too bad, right? How long could that take?

He was worried about the bar, even though they'd managed to keep all the appliances safe and dry. And he was terrified about the kitchen. The gas lines, the electrics, the grills, both of the walk-in refrigerators...he could get everything cleaned and repaired, but it was also possible he'd have to replace it all.

The inspector was taking his time. Jarlath had followed him around for almost half an hour of "hm" and "okay" and taking pictures and notes on an iPad, but he'd excused himself when he'd begun to feel queasy; he just couldn't take it.

He'd started to call Scott but didn't know if he and Jim were back from fishing yet. He'd tried to call Kate for a distraction, but she didn't pick up. He'd paced the length of his office a dozen times.

Maybe he should have taken Ezra up on his offer to be here with him.

Or Kate.

Or Scott.

He couldn't explain why, but he needed to be here alone. He needed the news, good or bad, to be his first so he could absorb it.

"Mister O'Connolly?"

Oh, fuck. The inspector. "I'm out by the bar."

"Ah. Found you." The man handed him a business card. "I'll email the report in the next day or two. In the meantime, I was able to turn your electricity back on. Your grill needs to be professionally cleaned before the gas can be, though. The walk-ins work, but I disconnected them again so you can have them serviced. The basement will need new wiring; it's all exposed which is no longer up to code, so I left those breakers off. The building structure is fine, your floors are fine, the bar survived well. I'd say you'll be up and running in a month or so."

Jar would swear he felt his heart stop. "In a...a month? I was hoping I could maybe serve from the bar this weekend at least?"

"Oh, no." The inspector shook his head and left, stopping to slap a bright-orange NO OCCUPANCY label on the door.

"Wait. What if I—"

"Sorry, sir. You'll get my report soon."

"Look. Hey." Jarlath put a hand on the guy's shoulder and got a glare in return. "Sorry." He pulled his hand away quickly. "Sorry, but...you don't get it. I need to get this place...I have employees, taxes, I lost all my inventory. I need to get running again. Soon. Now."

"I understand, sir. I do this for a living and as I'm sure you know, you're not the only flooded business in town. I'm sorry, but 'now' isn't possible. I'd count on a month."

"A month?" *A fucking month?* "Well, I do *this* for a living, only it's not making me a living right now because you just decorated my door with a goddamn orange sticker." He was frustrated, raising his voice.

"Don't wait for my report, just go ahead and schedule the work in the kitchen, that will take some time. Take care, now."

The inspector's patience was grating on Jarlath's last nerve. Couldn't he just fight? Yell? Give Jar something to be angry about? "Oh, sure. Yeah. You too, man. I hope you sleep well tonight."

The guy didn't look back, just got into his van and drove away.

"Ugh!" Jar tried to slam the door, forgetting that Ezra

had installed that gizmo last summer specifically to keep the heavy door from slamming. That wasn't satisfying, so he reached for a barstool and sent it flying across the empty dining room. *So fucking there.*

Yeah. That didn't make him feel better either. *Goddamn it.*

Fuck.

A month. A whole goddamn motherfucking month?

He stormed over and picked up the stool he'd thrown, and the bottom part of one of the legs went clattering to the floor. "Perfect," he said out loud to the empty room, then threw the stool on the floor again, hard enough to break another leg. Why not? He couldn't afford this place now anyway.

Fuck.

He wanted to...get into a fight. To punch something, or someone. He just needed to—

His phone rang, making him jump, and he fumbled it as he pulled it out of his pocket. "Goddamn it!" he shouted as he scooped it up off the floor. He made sure the screen looked okay before he answered it—one more expense he didn't need right now—and took a deep breath. It was Scott calling, and he didn't want to sound like a raving lunatic.

"Hey, Scott." *Breathe. Chill. You're not mad at him.*

"Hey, you. I've been thinking about you today. How did the inspection go?"

He bit his teeth together to keep from saying anything. How did it go? How did he answer that question? He was so fucking mad he could—

"Jar? You still there?"

"Yeah." He sighed, and he knew there was no way Scott hadn't heard it.

"You okay?"

"Yeah. Yeah, I'm—" *A wreck. Broke. Pissed off.* "I'm...you know what? Fuck this. What are you doing right now?"

"Now? Nothing I was—"

"Can you meet me at my place?" Jarlath marched over to the bar and grabbed his keys.

"Uh. Sure, I guess. What's up?"

He didn't want to answer questions. "I need to see you. Just get over there. Now."

"Whoa, okay. I-I can do that. I'll see you there."

Jarlath hung up the phone and locked up the pub.

20

————

Scott took "now" to heart. He gave Ma a kiss and rode like a bat out of hell to Jarlath's house. He didn't know for sure what was wrong, but Jar had seemed stressed on the phone, so he assumed the inspection hadn't gone well. That was kind of a worst-case scenario for the pub. He made himself relax as he passed the harbor and breathed in the cool sea air. He could handle this. A couple of beers, a shoulder to lean on, and maybe a fire in the firepit. He'd just let Jar vent, take him to bed after dinner, and they could sweat the rest of it out.

Stay cool, don't offer advice, keep the beer flowing.

He parked his motorcycle close to the house, so Jar would have room for his truck, and let himself in using the key in the fake rock under the pink azalea. That key had been there forever. Half the neighborhood knew how to get into Jar's house if they needed to. Jar's house was classic old Cape: there was an antique weather glass on the wall as you walked in the door that hung next to an ancient and out-of-date map of "Cape Cod and the Islands," a set of old boat fenders and a wooden buoy on the floor in the foyer, a pair of antique oars over the cabinets in the kitchen and a current tide chart on the fridge. He loved it for all of that—it was the house Jarlath had grown up in, and very little had changed about it.

Scott easily found two beers in the fridge and was opening them up when the screen door banged open and slammed closed again.

"Jar?"

Jar stormed into the kitchen, headed right for him. He held out a beer but Jar ignored it and kissed him, forcing him back against the fridge with the momentum. "Mm! Jar?" he managed to say around Jarlath's lips.

"Shh." Jar's hand covered his groin, hot palm searing through his jeans.

Jesus Christ, his balls responded before he could. "Jar. Just…give me a second to catch up."

"Okay." Jar took a beer and swallowed half of it, then set it down hard on the counter. He took Scott's bottle too. "Caught up now?"

"What's going on?"

Jar rubbed him with firm pressure, and his body responded despite his complete confusion, obviously understanding much more of what was going on than he did. Not that this was complicated, he supposed.

Jar's fingers opened his button and fly. "Want you."

"Okay. Cool, okay. You can have me." Fuck, his cock had gone from zero to party time in seconds. He tried to clear his head enough to think about this, whether it was a good idea. "Jar, are you okay?"

"Don't talk, Scott." Jar pushed his shirt up and attacked a nipple with killer suction.

"Fuck, Jar." He pushed his hips into Jarlath's hand and arched to those evil, hungry lips. Did that count as talking?

"Yeah, man. That's the idea." Jarlath let him go and tugged a rubber out of his wallet. "Right here."

"Here?"

"Scott. Shut up and fuck me." Jar dropped his jeans, and Scott gave up thinking. Jarlath's ass was round and pale where it never saw the sun, and the way Jar was arching for him was as beautiful as it was obscene. He pulled his cock out and suited up, the touch of his own hand enough to make him gasp.

"Lube?"

"Just do it."

Jesus. Why was being ordered around so fucking hot? He lined up, his aching cock pushing gently against Jar's pretty little puckered hole. "Fuck, baby."

"More."

He nodded. "Just making sure—fuck!" His eyes crossed and his knees nearly buckled out from under him as Jar pushed back and took him in fast and deep, arms braced on the kitchen counter.

"More! More, Scott. Fuck me."

His body had left his mind behind and was taking orders like a seasoned Marine. He gripped Jar's hips and took him hard and fast, hips rolling and ass clenching with the effort.

Jar reached across the counter and splayed his fingers out across the backsplash for leverage. "Yes, fuck, Scott. More."

"I—Jar…" He raked in a harsh breath.

"More, Scott! Harder."

Okay, what the fuck? Jar had gone off the fucking deep end, but he didn't think about it, just did what he was told. He reached over Jar and gripped one shoulder, and his other hand found Jarlath's cock just below counter height and tightened around it.

"Oh fuck, oh God." Jar ducked his head and exhaled heavily.

"Good?"

"Yes. Fuck, yes."

"Close?" He gritted his teeth and dug deeper, finding another gear, tearing into Jarlath and telling his balls to hold the hell off for another minute.

"Yes, yes..."

The kitchen filled with filthy sounds, grunts and moans and cursing, as he pushed Jarlath through the testosterone cloud and off a fucking psychotic cliff. Jar shouted and shot, the scent filling Scott's nostrils and shattering that last bit of self-control he'd been clinging to.

Blood roared in his ears as he came, trembling, hips sputtering awkwardly through his climax. He braced a hand on the counter edge to keep from falling as he gulped air and shook his head to clear it.

Jar was breathing hard, and Scott heard him moan as they parted. He threw the condom into the kitchen garbage and tugged his jeans up, then coaxed Jarlath off the counter and into his arms. The way Jar kissed him still felt a little desperate, and he stroked a hand over Jar's hair, whispering "shhh," as he held him close.

It took a bit for the storm to pass, but as all storms do, it did eventually let them go. Jarlath straightened up and caught his eye. "Thank you."

"Are you okay?"

"No. I'm better now, but no."

He eyed Jar carefully. "Jarlath, what the fuck is going on?" They were both still a little winded as they watched each other. Jarlath finally tucked himself back into his jeans, grabbed both beers, and handed him one. "Thanks. Hey. Talk to me?"

"I really don't want to talk." Jar took another huge swig of beer. "The inspector said it's going to be a month before..." Jar choked on the next word and tried again. "Before I can...open."

"What?" *Oh. Fuck.* "A month?"

Jar nodded and swiped at his eyes with the heel of his hand. "Fuck. A fucking month, Scott."

Okay. He'd had a plan, right? Before the deranged tornado came bursting into the kitchen? He'd been ready for this.

What the fuck was the plan again?

Oh, yeah. Chill. Breathe. Got it.

He pulled Jarlath back into his arms and just held him.

"I'm going to lose it. It was my dad's place, I promised him I'd keep it going, and now I'm going to lose it."

"No. You're not. Shit, Jar, if your dad were here now, if he'd seen all that water..."

"He'd fix it. He'd know what to do, who to call, and he'd just fix it."

"I bet not. I bet he'd be freaking out too, and then he'd calm down and think. He'd sit with the numbers and figure something out."

Jar sighed, shoulders drooping against him.

"Listen, I know about losing a business. You're not there yet."

Jar leaned a bit more and blinked at him. "You don't think?"

"Seriously. You have some options. We tried everything, trust me. There's money out there." Wait a minute. Could he actually be helpful here? *Holy shit.*

"I just need this month covered. Rent, repairs, some startup cash for when I can finally open up."

"It's just money, Jar. We'll find it."

"Wait. We?"

He nodded. There were SBA loans, grants, insurance, investors, fundraisers? "Yes, we. If you'll let me."

"I need help, Scott. Goddamn it, I hate to ask, I hate having to."

He heard that. The bar might be all dried out now, but Jarlath was drowning. "You didn't ask, I offered. And I think I can actually help. For real."

Jarlath took a huge breath, chest heaving and shoulders lifting, then blew it out in a rough sigh. "Okay. Okay, thank you. Jesus, I'm glad you came home. I mean—fuck, I mean, I'm sorry about your company, I really am. I didn't mean—I'm just really glad you're here."

He'd felt like he was coming home with his tail between his legs, but he didn't anymore. He was glad to be home. He belonged here. "The west coast was fun, and beautiful, but it never felt like home."

"Oh yeah, that's right. What did you miss again? Quahogs? Little necks?"

"Ha-ha."

"Portuguese bread. Oh! Saltwater taffy? Tourists."

"Definitely the tourists. They don't have any of those in San Francisco." He kissed Jarlath to shut him up, chuckling against Jar's lips. "I missed the people. And Ma. And you."

Jarlath rolled his eyes. "I wasn't fishing for—"

"I know." He wasn't one for taking bait anyway.

Jar finished his beer and sat the empty bottle on the counter. "I'm sorry I attacked you like some lunatic."

"You are?" He shrugged. "I don't think I am."

"No?" Jar glanced at him.

"Are you blushing?"

"Fuck, no." Jar shook his head and rolled his eyes.

"Man, you came storming in here, guns blazing, and just

shorted me right the hell out. It was crazy. And hot. You were fucking hot."

"I didn't want to think. I just wanted to feel something good."

"Well, that was good. Insane, but really good." And to hell with that little voice in the back of his head that was telling him he'd kind of been used and reminding him how much he wanted them to be an out-there couple.

He'd wrestle with that later.

"It was, huh? God, I needed you."

I needed *you*, not I needed *that*. There it was, right? He didn't want to push the issue right now, but somewhere under all of Jarlath's stress and reluctance, there was something real there. He knew it.

And he intended to hold on to it.

"I'm here for you, Jar. I promise."

Jar leaned on him heavily. "Thank you."

"Of course. This is a good thing we're doing, Jar. You and me. It's good."

Jar nodded against him and gave him a squeeze.

"So, firepit? Grilled cheese, maybe?"

"S'mores. Bug spray."

He snorted. "Sounds perfect. You get the bread, I'll get the cheese."

Chill. No advice. Beer. Poke at the fire a while and make some plans to go fishing or take the ferry to Martha's Vineyard. Keep Jar's mind off the pub for a few hours. He could do this.

21

"Hello?"

"Jarlath, it's Jim. Kate just told me about the inspector. I'm so sorry, that sucks."

Jarlath sat down on the floor in his office with a sigh. He'd just finished laying the new carpet, and he could use the break. "Yeah. Thanks, Jim. I'll get through it." He wasn't sure how, but that was what you said, right? *Sound positive, don't put your shit on other people.*

"Of course you will. She and Scott are at the house talking right now."

"Scott is talking to—" So that was how Kate knew. And "at the house" meant Ma's house, so Ma knew now too. He sighed.

"It's cool, Jarlath. He's asking her to help with a fundraiser."

He blinked. "He is?"

"Yeah, they're planning something right there on the beach. A clambake and a bonfire, a band, a raffle...they're dreaming up all kinds of stuff."

"Wow."

"Party planning is right up Kate's alley, you know."

"I forgot. A fundraiser. Are they sure this is a good idea? I mean, lots of folks were underwater; there's not much to go around."

"Downtown wasn't hit like you were, and besides, it'll be fun. It's going to be a big party. They'll make it worth attending. I'm already thinking about what the club can do."

He swallowed down a little lump of emotion and nodded. "Thanks, Jim. I just need a month. I need a month and some cash to get rolling again."

"Scott's got this, Jar. He does. He has some great ideas. Just concentrate on getting the work done."

"I'm on it. I just finished recarpeting the office." He wasn't sure what to do next.

"Good. It'll come together. Let me know if there's anything you need."

"Will do. Thanks so much for calling."

"Take care." Jim hung up the phone, and Jarlath stared at the blank screen for a minute, picturing Scott and Kate putting their heads together. Their blond heads like Ma's, and their wide shoulders like Ned's. Kate had been a party planner before the boys came along—he'd completely forgotten. Maybe Scott really did know what he was doing.

God, he hoped so. He was cruising on a wing and a prayer right now.

He stood and found his water bottle, sipping as he walked the edges of the room, inspecting his work. He'd done a pretty damn good job.

"Hey, it's looking good in here." Ezra appeared in his doorway with a cardboard box in his hands.

"Thanks. New paint, and I just finished the carpet. What's in the box?"

"Oh. Lunch. And all the pictures you took down. I found

them in the pile of stuff you'd brought in from your truck." Ezra set the box on the floor. "I figured we could put them back up."

He smiled. "Yeah. I guess I'm about ready. Thanks. Will you help me with my new desk?"

"You got it. Is that what I saw out on the dance floor?"

"Yeah, it's actually not as heavy as it looks, we're just going to have to turn it on its side I think to get it through the door."

"Okay. Let's do it."

It took the two of them about half an hour to get the desk in place, his chair, the new file cabinet, and the couple of pieces he was able to rescue from the flood: a long console table that ran along the wall behind his desk and a pair of leather guest chairs he'd put up on top of Dad's desk to keep them dry. He was glad to have those, especially since Dad's desk couldn't be saved.

They hung all his dad's old pictures pretty much exactly where they'd always been, plus added one of him standing in front of the bar the morning before the storm hit, just standing there with all the sandbags and the windows boarded up.

"That one's kind of depressing, huh?" Ezra looked at it closely. "You look exhausted."

"Well, I don't think so. To me it's a reminder that we did everything we could to take care of the place, you know?"

"Oh." Ezra nodded. "Yeah. I like that."

There was a knock on his door, one of the workmen who was there servicing the refrigerators, and he excused himself to go deal with that. It turned out to be good news, but by the time he got back, lunch was on his desk with a note from Ezra that read, "Looks great in here. Call if you need me. See you tomorrow."

He pulled out his phone and texted Ezra to thank him for his help and for lunch. It was small gestures like this that were getting him through this.

"Is that a grinder? I'm starving." Scott strolled in, looking handsome and smiling, hands in his pockets. He smiled too and took a deep breath. It felt as if Scott had brought new air in with him.

"Yes. Let's share it."

"Hey, it's looking great in here. You have the pictures up already?"

"Ezra stopped by to help. He's such a good guy. A good friend." Ezra was the only person he really trusted the pub with—well, and Nadine. She'd been texting and keeping in touch, too, but her parents' house had a tree go through the roof, so she'd had that to deal with and hadn't been able to be here much since that first weekend.

"Well, it looks great. I like the new desk."

"Thanks." He handed Scott half his sandwich. "Jim called and said you were conspiring with Kate."

Scott rolled his eyes. "A little. Mostly she was running with a fundraiser idea I pitched to her. She has some good thoughts. Did he tell you I met with a banker?"

"No..." But he already knew he wasn't interested.

"Yeah, he has an investment firm, he's offered to help you get a loan."

He snorted. "Investment firms don't do loans."

"Well, no. His firm would guarantee it for you."

"Yeah, I don't know about that, Scott." He needed cash, but he wasn't sure yet if he even wanted a loan.

Scott nodded. "I understand. I did contact someone about an SBA loan and you likely qualify, but I asked around about getting a conventional loan too, and that's going to be hard since you're not up and running. These guys offered to invest too, if you—"

Oh, bullshit. "You mean *buy*. I know these people. They're always trying to get their hands on my property." It was prime real estate—directly across from the beach, right near The Wharf hotel and the resorts, right at the finish line for the Falmouth Road Race.

"I got you, Jar. I told them you weren't looking for a business partner, and you definitely weren't selling."

"Thanks. I'll think about it." He thought about it. *No.*

"Well, it's there if you need it. He said he might come by to talk to you."

"Great. Tell me more about the fundraiser?"

They ate their sandwiches, and Scott told him all about what Kate had proposed, assuming she could get all the permits and the volunteers she needed for her beach party. A band, games, a clambake, a bonfire...all donated and run by volunteers. They'd charge a cover to get in, and after that everything but the alcohol would be free. At the end of the day, the money would cover the charges for the permits, security, all that stuff, and the rest would go to his start-up costs for the bar.

"I'm really—I hate having to ask for help, Scott."

"Again, you didn't ask, Jar. I offered. And Kate is actually excited about planning the fundraiser. She and Jim have wanted to help out, they just didn't know how. I think we all feel that way, even Ma. I'm glad to have found some way to be useful."

"Well, I'm grateful. I am. Thank you."

"You're welcome."

They finished their sandwiches in silence, and Jarlath was amazed that it didn't feel awkward or uncomfortable. He was happy to be sitting with Scott. And still stunned too.

He'd known he'd probably run into Scott again one day, maybe at a wedding or a funeral, but he'd never expected Scott to come home from California for good. He'd written off the idea entirely, but without any real closure, he'd never dealt with his feelings. He hadn't had a name for them then; he'd been too young, too closeted, too...new. He'd just buried them.

The day their eyes had locked in the pub, though— Scott's still so blue like the summer sky—those feelings had all come flooding back, high and deep, and he had no idea *how* to deal with them now.

"So...they're working in the kitchen?" Scott's question pulled him out of his head.

"Hm?" Jar looked up, still holding the last bite of his sandwich. "Oh. Yeah. The crew managed to save the walk-ins, but they needed service. The gas lines are all being replaced, but the ovens and the grill will be okay too. I'm so relieved."

"Oh, great. You needed a win, huh?"

He nodded. "I so did. I can't imagine what all of that would have cost me, even with insurance." He had flood insurance, and the insurance company would come through eventually. Hopefully that would help him pay off whatever loan he might need to take in the short term.

"The sandwich was good, thanks for sharing."

"Ezra brought it. There's always too much food for one person."

"Well, do you want to put me to work? What's next on your list?"

"Um." He thought about that; there was so much. What should be next? "I need to sand the bar so I can refinish it, and I need to get the computer and the Wi-Fi up and running in here. Now that the electricity is on."

"Okay, point me to the sandpaper."

"There's a box down cellar."

"Ooh, the newly renovated, shiny cellar? I haven't seen it yet."

"No? They did a nice job. Drylok paint, new wiring, new pump system, and they cleaned the metal shelving and replaced the no-slip treads on the stairs."

"Geez. That's a lot of new."

"No shit. I paid the up-front deposit, but that bill is going to hurt when it gets here. And it's half what the kitchen is costing me. Fuck, I don't want to think about it."

"Yep. No more thinking." Scott gathered up their garbage and put it into the bag it all came in. "Wi-Fi, you said?"

"Yeah, and the computer."

"See? No time to think. You have work to do. Give me your phone." Scott held out his hand.

"My—why?"

Scott rolled his eyes. "Just give it to me."

He pulled his phone out and handed it over.

"Thank you." Scott unlocked it by holding it up to his face, making him laugh. A second later, there was music playing—R.E.M. Scott sat the phone down on his desk. "Sing along when you start to think too hard."

"You're too much."

"I'm not kidding. Sing. And work. You're going to need that computer up and running so you can place some orders soon."

"I hope so."

"You will. Soon. You watch." Scott reached for him and pulled him in for a quick, hard kiss. "Trust me."

"I do." He blinked at Scott, feeling a little dazed. "Another?"

Scott nodded and kissed him more slowly. By the time it was over, he felt like maybe he could breathe again.

"I'll be sanding if you need me."

"Thank you so much, Scott."

"Anytime. Anything." Scott gave him a wink and disappeared through the office door.

God, he wanted to believe that. He was trying. Scott had come home and been everything he wanted. But it wasn't just Scott; he was having a hard time believing anything right now.

"Found the sandpaper. That is one sexy cellar!" Scott called down the hall. He almost didn't hear over the R.E.M. He laughed and got to work too.

22

"Scott. Look at all of this..." Jar sounded completely awed, and rightfully so. The parking lot was packed, and the beach was covered in booths and people, many of whom had begun to gather near a small stage near the hotel.

"Jar! Scotty!"

Scott elbowed Jar and pointed to the beach entrance. "There she is. Hey, Kate!"

"Hey! It's about time you guys got here, the band is going to start soon."

"Sorry." Scott gave her a hug. "We were refinishing the bar and ran a little long."

Kate smiled brightly. "Oh, is that done now?"

"Yes. It looks great." He and Jar had worked hard, and Jar was super proud of it. "It just needs to dry for a couple of days. Wait until you see it."

"Yeah. Jar has it roped off like a crime scene." He rolled his eyes.

Jar snorted at him. "Well? No one will touch it now, will they?"

"Nope," he agreed. "No, they won't. They might be charged with tampering with evidence."

"Ha!" Kate laughed. "Good one."

"Shut up, Kate. You're supposed to be on my side," Jar protested.

What, now? "Your side? She's my sister..."

Kate sighed, exasperated. "All right, time to go in and have some fun, you two."

"Can't wait. Thank you so much. This is amazing." Jar kissed her cheek and walked right in.

Scott followed his lead, but Kate grabbed his arm. "Hey. That's fifteen bucks, brother."

"What? Jar just—"

"Jarlath is free. Ma is also free. Everyone else pays, even you." Kate was dead serious.

"Even Jim?"

"Even Jim. Even *me*." She raised an eyebrow, daring him to argue.

He laughed. "Oh well, as long as Ma got in free." He handed Kate a fifty. "That's for me and Ma and Jar too. Jim can cover you."

She squeezed his hand. "You're a good man. Now, go spend some more money."

"I'm on it!" He chuckled and followed after Jar, who was already surrounded by people.

"Hey, Scott." Ezra stuck out a hand and Scott shook it.

"Whoa, look at this, the whole gang is here, huh?"

Jarlath started pointing to people. "Scott, this is Ezra's wife, Lisa, and she is holding baby June. Have you met Benny? And this is Celia, and their brand-new little Michael who, you might remember, decided to show up on Labor Day."

"Yep. Celia went into labor on Labor Day. How could I

forget?" He shook hands with everyone. "You're the reason Jarlath trusts me behind the bar again."

"I'm here!"

Scott turned and waved to Nadine, who was jogging across the sand.

"Hey, Boss. Scott. Oh my God, everybody brought babies!" Everyone chuckled, and Nadine blushed. "Sorry. I just love babies."

"It's really good to see you guys. If you're ready to get back to work, I'm going to need some help soon restocking and polishing up the place." Everyone agreed they'd be there, and Jar looked relieved. "I'll be in touch, okay? I think I better make the rounds a little."

He and Jarlath wandered, shaking hands here and there until they ran into Ma and Jim. "Hey, Ma."

"Scotty. Jarlath." They each kissed a cheek. "An embarrassment of riches," she joked, smiling and blushing. "My boys."

"Are you having a good time, Ma?"

"Oh, yes. The little lobster poppers over there are to die for, and there are stuffies over there where the grill is. And I have the most marvelous iced tea." She proudly held up a cup with a straw in it.

"We heard the band was going to be starting up soon, though, so Ma decided it was time to go. I'll take her home and come back."

"Thank you, Jim. It's good to see you, Ma."

"Jarlath, Scott. I want you to come to dinner Saturday evening. Dad will be with us, and Jim and Kate...I'd like it to be a family thing."

"Of course, Ma. We'll be there." Jar was quick to answer.

Scott agreed. "I'll help with the grill, Jim." Not that Jim needed help, but he liked to offer.

"Fantastic."

"Well, see you boys then. Have a great time." Ma gave them a wave and walked off again, carefully making her way through the sand with Jim at her elbow.

"I guess we have plans Saturday." Jar winked at him.

He nodded. "You don't say no to Ma."

"Nope. Never."

Jar stopped them as they wandered past the beer booth. "Oh. Did you ask if I wanted a beer? Yes, please," Jarlath got right in line.

"Oh, I absolutely did." Scott grinned and pulled out his wallet.

The band started their set, and down the beach people whistled and applauded. He didn't recognize them, but Jar did.

"Oh! She got Float Your Goat to play! Do you know these guys? I think they might have showed up after you left town. They're local and they're really good. Dash, their lead singer, he's seriously talented. So soulful, and then he kind of rocks out. Love him."

He hadn't even heard of them. Crazy, the things he'd missed.

They got their beers, which he paid for even though they tried to give Jarlath both of them for free, and wandered some more. He didn't think much of the game booths, but Jar was kind of lingering, moving slowly, watching people play. That made him want to be *that* guy— the one that won the huge teddy bear for his girlfriend. Jarlath needed a giant teddy bear like a hole in the head, and they were scarce anyway, but he stopped at a booth all the same.

"Oh, Jar." He took Jar's elbow. "I am going to win you something."

Jar looked at him skeptically. "Yeah, sure. These things are always rigged."

"I've got this. It's just a ring toss. I'm going to win you that inflatable lobster."

Jarlath laughed. "You're never gonna do it."

"No? You wanna bet?"

Jar raised an eyebrow. "Sure. I win...you have to dance on the bar the night we open."

Oh, good Lord. He'd better fucking win. "Okay. And if I win, you have to hang the lobster behind the bar and tell everyone on opening day that I won it for you."

Jar shook his head. "Deal. There's no way."

"Challenge accepted." He was determined now, if only because Jarlath was so sure he couldn't do it. He stepped up to the counter and handed a couple of dollars over in exchange for a handful of rings. "The lobster. You see that? It's going home with you."

"We'll see."

He shook his head and tossed a ring. It bounced off one bottle and then another, and then three more before falling between them, and settling on none of them. "Damn. This is harder than it looks."

"Told you." Jarlath sang playfully.

He rolled his eyes. "Your confidence in me is overwhelming. Okay. Here we go." He tossed the next one and it was so close. The third one had no chance at all, but the fourth...

"No...no way."

"Ha! Yes!" He threw both hands in the air like he was a fucking champ. "Did you see that? Did you? Mister Told You So? Huh?"

"I saw it," Jarlath mumbled.

"What was that?" Oh, he was going to milk this for everything it was worth.

"I saw it," Jar repeated, louder this time. "Unbelievable, but you did it."

"Damn right I did. I am the man! Yes. Rar!" He was making a fool of himself, he knew, but it was only to embarrass Jar even more.

"Okay. I get the point. Geez."

"Good." He settled down, feeling smug. "The inflatable lobster, please, sir."

He was handed a plastic lobster in a flimsy cardboard box, and he waved it in Jar's face. "Uh-huh. One lobster. And everyone is going to know who won it for you."

"I can't believe it. Nobody wins those games. Nobody ever."

"Nobody but me. I am *that* lucky. I got the lobster, and you." He smiled at Jarlath, wanting a kiss so bad, but not sure if Jarlath would go for it with all these people around.

"Scotty." Jarlath smiled at him and took his hand.

Hey. Okay, that was...good. Something good. He didn't push for the kiss yet; he didn't want to blow this moment. Instead, he just squeezed Jar's fingers and smiled back. "*Lobstah*."

"You betcha."

They both laughed.

"Mister O'Connolly?"

They both turned, and he had to assume Jarlath was as confused as he was. Nobody called Jar "Mister" anything. He was Jarlath to anyone he cared about.

"Can I help you?" Jar asked, sounding caught between curious and skeptical.

"Actually, I think I can help you. My name is Perry Stevens, I'm from Robbins and Carson in Hyannis and—"

Oh, boy.

"No, thank you."

"Mister O'Connolly, I think you should hear me out. My firm has—"

"My father was Mister O'Connolly and he's gone, so I don't think you're going to get very far talking to him. I'm Jarlath, and I am having fun at a fundraiser right now."

Ooh. Jar was already testy.

The guy went on, undaunted. "Well, maybe we could set up an appointment for next week. We know you're strapped for cash, and I think if you'd consider an investment from us, we could get you back on your feet even better than before."

"Better than before? It was great before. I don't need better. I need what I had, and that's what this fundraiser is about."

"You're going to need a loan, at least, Mister O'Con— Jarlath. But an investment would mean that you don't have to pay us anything in return. We'd let you run the place your way, we'd just help you with some decision making."

"*Let* me...excuse me?" Jar was full-on pissed now. "What makes you think I'd want an arrangement like that? It's my pub, my father's pub left to me to manage, and I'll run it on my own and as I please. I'd rather close the doors than sell out to the likes of you."

There was a moment of silence, and Scott was just about to step in and chase the asshole off when he started talking again.

"Suit yourself. When you close, we'll be right there waiting and we will run it entirely our way after that. Your father's pub will become *our* nightclub."

"Not in a hundred fucking years." Jar took a step toward the guy and Scott moved in.

"Enough. Let's go, Mister Stevens." Scott crowded the guy, forcing him to back up a step and turn around. He was going to see this asshole out himself. "Time to go. And if you harass Jarlath one more time—here, on the phone, at the pub, you'll have me to deal with—am I clear?"

"Are you threatening me?"

He snorted. "I'm just trying to help you."

They reached the entrance and he made sure Stevens walked through the gate, and he turned to Kate. "Don't let him back in, okay?"

"Is everything okay?"

"Yes. Jar's having a great time. That guy was trying to ruin it for him."

Kate gave him a nod. "Well, then he won't be getting in. I promise."

"Thank you. This is a great party, Kate. It's amazing. You're amazing." He looked at Kate, his big sister. "You know, I don't say that enough, but it's true. You're an amazing woman."

"Wow." Kate beamed at him and kissed his cheek. "Thank you, baby brother. Now, go find Jar and make sure he has some fun."

"Will do!" He waved and jogged off.

Jar wasn't where he'd left him, and he wasn't near the food either, so Scott pulled out his phone and texted.

Where did you go?

Listening to the band. Far side by the fence.

Scott raised his head and looked around, heading for the fence, where he finally spotted Jar leaning back and listening. He leaned next to Jar and watched the band too for a few minutes, letting the dust settle between them a little. He slid his fingers over until they touched Jar's, and Jar took his hand instantly.

He tucked Jar's hand against his thigh. "Are you okay?"

Jar nodded. "I just don't need assholes to make this worse."

"I regret getting in contact with them."

"Oh, don't worry about that. He'd already left me two voice mails before you'd contacted anybody."

"Jesus. They didn't even tell me."

"Well, they wouldn't. They're in the business of buying up everything on the Cape. They probably appreciated the tip."

He sighed. "Well, I hope I didn't make it worse."

Jar looked over at him. "Don't worry about it. You've been so helpful, especially when I start thinking I'll never get there. You just...remind me what's important."

"Jar." He raised their hands and looked at them, tracing Jar's fingers with his other hand. "I'd really like to kiss you right now. I know you want to keep things private, and there are a lot of people around. I get maybe it makes you uncomfortable, but I—"

"Jesus Christ, Scott. Just kiss me."

He turned his head abruptly and stared at Jarlath. "Yeah?"

"There is nothing romantic about reminding me of all the reasons you shouldn't."

He grinned. "You're a little shit when you want to be." He followed that with a kiss, a safe one for children and prime time, but still a very real, very public kiss.

And the crazy thing was, he was pretty sure nobody even noticed.

Jar smiled at him as the band played a new song. "Oh! This is my favorite of theirs." Jar pulled him into the crowd. Everyone was dancing, and as Dash began to sing, Jar swayed from side to side with his arms in the air. Scott moved up behind him and swayed with him, resting his hands on Jar's hips.

He'd signed on for one hell of a ride with Jarlath, but he was going to roll with it. He had no intention of getting off it. Right now, he was the happiest man on the planet.

23

"You guys are still here?"

"We've been helping people pack up and clean up," Jarlath said, going to Kate to give her a hug.

"You don't have to help, Jar. This day is for you."

"I know it is, and I'm just—it's the least I can do. Honestly. I'm seriously overwhelmed by all of this."

"Well, I don't have exact figures yet obviously, but you're going to be even more overwhelmed when you see what we brought in today."

His heart beat hard in his chest as he allowed himself to think maybe this was going to be okay. "Kate, I can't thank you enough for...everything."

"You just did. But you know what's neat? Everyone said yes the first time I asked. The band, the games, the food trucks, they all volunteered their time and donated their profits. The town didn't charge us for the permits; the Wharf was cool about letting us use their stage. It's been amazing. So it's not just me, everyone wanted to help."

He felt hot tears at the corner of his eyes and brushed them away, shaking his head.

"Hey. I know, it's huge. Everyone knows you, they know you appreciate them, or they wouldn't have done it." Scott put an arm around his shoulders, and he nodded. He knew. He just couldn't get the words out right now.

"Why don't you guys go on home? We're almost done here."

He shook his head. "Soon. Thanks, Kate. Thank you again."

Kate kissed his cheek. "I love you like a brother, Jar. And we drop everything for family. You guys get home safe." She kissed Scott too, then touched his arm and left.

Scott kissed his shoulder. "Why don't we head out, Jar?"

"Soon. I want to—can we go sit?" He needed to process all of this. He needed to watch the beach empty and go quiet. He didn't want this incredible day to be over yet.

"Sure. It's a beautiful night, right?" Scott took his hand.

"A perfect night, to top off a perfect day."

They started walking, and Scott made some small talk. "You were right about the band, they're so good."

"Maybe I'll have them come play for the reopening."

"Oh, that would be a great idea." Scott found them a bench facing the water and sitting in the shadow of the sea wall. It was dark and quiet, people walking by above would probably have no idea they were there.

"Good spot."

"Quiet spot, I thought. Good place to rest for a minute, talk, think."

"Don't you think I think too much already?"

Scott laughed. "I do, in fact. We both think way too much. But you're the boss, right? You have to be a few steps ahead of everyone."

He sighed. "I don't feel like I'm ahead of you. I feel like I'm a mile behind all the time."

"Shit." Scott put a hand on his knee. "I'm sorry. I don't mean to rush you."

"No. No, you're not. It's not actually that you're rushing me, Scott. It's that I'm dragging my feet. I've just been feeling so off-balance. I'm worried about the pub, about Dad, Ma, money...it's been hard to focus on this. On you."

"I understand, it's okay."

Scott had been so generous—with his help, his time, his patience.

"I appreciate that, but it's really not okay." He found Scott's hand and took it between both of his. "You've been the best thing about all of this. I don't know how you managed it, but you dropped back into my life out of nowhere, just in time for a fucking hurricane, almost like...I don't know, a guardian angel or something. Like you knew I was going to need help. Need...you."

"I didn't know, obviously, but I'm glad I've been here to help. Knowing how it's played out now, I'm not sorry about the timing either."

"I would have made it through this somehow without you. I know I would have. I have great people surrounding me and family and...I'd have made it eventually." He was strong, and he was his father's son after all. He'd have figured it out somehow. "But the pub isn't even going to open for two more weeks, and I already know it'll be okay. And that's because of you. It's still stressful in a lot of ways, but I'm not worried or anxious because...because I know you're here, and I know you can help. You *have* helped."

He dropped his head to Scott's shoulder, and Scott put an arm around him. "That's what I want. I want you to feel like I'm solid, because I am. I'm home, Jar. For good, you know? For you, for Dad, for Ma. This is where I need to be."

Jarlath sighed again, working out the right words before he said them. "Will you—I want you to move in with me."

He heard Scott's breath catch, felt Scott's heart start to beat faster. He hoped that was a good sign, but just in case he added, "Please."

"Yeah? You want me to? For real?" Scott's voice was soft, he sounded surprised.

"Yes. For real."

"Because I would love to. I really would."

Jar smiled and stretched up to kiss Scott's jaw. "Good. That settles it then. You think Ma will be okay?"

"Are you kidding? I can't wait to tell her. She's suggested a couple of times that I should look for a place of my own, but I've been hoping—" Scott chuckled, the sound adorable and embarrassed. "I've been hoping for this."

He grinned, pleased with that answer. "Why? You can't handle sleeping in that twin bed anymore?"

"I think it's all the yearbooks in the bookcase and the nautical bedspread."

"Not a lot has changed in that room, it's true."

"Nope. Not very much at all. Except that I got bigger."

"Mmm." Feeling daring, he slid a hand over Scott's fly. "A lot bigger."

"Oh, fuck." Scott's cock reacted quickly to his touch, and the soft little moan made Jarlath blush all over and his heart race. "Jesus, Jar. A week ago you wouldn't hold my hand in public."

"This isn't really public. Nobody can see us here in the shadows." He rubbed a little more firmly, tracing the hard bulge under Scott's khaki shorts.

Scott took a breath and he could tell it was work for him to whisper. "No?"

"No. But they'll hear you, for sure."

"Jar."

"Shh." He lowered Scott's fly and fished out that lovely, thick cock.

"Mm." Scott was biting his lips together to keep quiet, and it made him grin. He felt daring and young, remembering the teenager that had done this many times before. But he wasn't fumbling and trying to get it right anymore. He knew what Scott wanted and how to make him crazy.

And Scott was going to have to keep very quiet anyway.

"Shh," he said again as he slid off the bench and settled between Scott's knees.

"Wait. Jar." Scott scootched farther back on the bench like he was trying to get away, but he just moved in closer, ignoring the protest. "Jar."

"That's my name. Now hush."

24

"You drive like a little old lady."

"Well, it's a little old lady's car, Dad." Scott kept his eyes on the road. Dad had done nothing but complain since Scott picked him up. He kept telling himself to breathe, that Dad was just anxious about the car ride and would be better once he saw Ma.

"Don't let her hear you say that."

"No, sir. That would be rude."

"I'm glad you still have some manners."

Scott turned the corner, counting to ten. "Jim's making chicken on the grill, and corn."

"I can't eat corn on the cob."

"We'll cut it off for you. The boys don't like it on the cob either. They're looking forward to seeing you."

"Who is?"

Oh, man. "The boys, Dad. Kate's boys."

"Oh, yes. Uh..."

"Aiden," he prompted gently.

"Right. Aiden and the baby."

"Noah. He's almost three."

Dad looked at him, then looked out the window again. "Is Jarlath going to be there?"

He took a breath, trying to be cool, but remembering how Jim had called Jarlath "the golden boy."

"Yes. He's coming straight from the pub."

"Oh. Good. It will be nice to see him."

It was bad form to get into an argument with your aging, forgetful father a few minutes before a family dinner, but he so wanted to. Dad had a way of making him feel like an idiot, or just plain invisible.

"Well, at least you won't get a speeding ticket."

"Dad. Give it a rest. We're almost there."

He was counting to ten for the third time as he turned into the driveway. Kate came out and meet them at the car to help Scott get Dad into his chair.

"Sorry we're late, Scotty is a terrible driver."

Kate looked at him over Dad's head. "Oh, it was a good drive, huh?"

"Very entertaining." He rolled his eyes and Kate laughed.

"Where do you want to be, Dad?" Kate bent to Dad's level once they got him in the house. "In the kitchen with Ma, out on the deck with Jim grilling, or in the living room with the boys?"

"I should say hello to Mother first, I think."

Scott winked at Kate. That was proof that Dad was still in there. He might be an ornery old coot, but he adored Ma and still treated her like a queen. When he remembered her.

"You got it." Kate took Dad in to see Ma, and Scott stood in the foyer to breathe for a minute. He and Jarlath had planned to tell everyone tonight that he was moving into Jarlath's house. He didn't think anyone would be shocked, but he worried about leaving Ma here on her own. He'd be close, though, ten minutes away was all, and Kate and Jim weren't much farther away. It was just that for all her talk about him finding a place of his own, he didn't like the idea of Ma being lonely without Dad in the house.

He looked out the window but there was still no sign of Jar, so he headed out back to see about the grill with Jim.

"Hey! Dad get here all right?"

"I managed not to strangle him, even after the third time he criticized my driving."

Jim nodded, looking impressed. "You are a man of valor."

They both laughed. "The chicken looks great."

"It's my secret recipe. Soy, garlic, cilantro, some lime, and brown sugar. It grills up nice." Jim looked proud of himself.

"It's not a secret if you tell me what's in it, Jim."

"It's not a secret anyway, I think I got it online." Jim chuckled and sipped his beer. "Getting chilly, huh? It's really fall now. Aiden's been talking about Halloween costumes."

"Oh, God. We're not there yet, are we?"

"Not quite. But close enough for chocolate lovers to start getting excited."

"Oh, so this Halloween talk is Kate's fault." Kate was a chocoholic.

"Nope. I didn't say a thing. Not me." Jim winked at him. "So how's the pub shaping up?"

"It's just about ready to open. Jar's been working his ass off, and his bartenders have been there, getting the place organized and placing orders for liquor and whatever else they need. Jar's chomping at the bit. He just needs the inspector to come back and clear the place to open."

"When is he coming?"

"Sometime this week, supposedly. Jar's losing his mind, though, without a firm date."

"How long after it passes inspection before Jar will be able to open?"

"Hopefully not long. He won't need to stock too much more for the bar, just fresh stuff, and he could even open just that part while he gets in the supplies for the kitchen."

"So frustrating."

"Yeah. It's okay, though. Kate's fundraiser was off the hook, and Jar was able to get a loan to tide him over until he has some cash coming in again. It's small, but it's enough."

"That's great. I'm glad to hear it. I'll keep my fingers"—Jim was interrupted by a commotion in the house—"crossed for him."

Scott peered through the glass sliders that led into the house. "That's probably him."

"Go ahead, man. I got this."

"Thanks. It smells great." He clapped Jim on the shoulder and went inside.

"Oh. There he is! Scott, come here." Ma's smile was bright and happy, and she waved him over. "Go on, Jar, tell him."

Jarlath looked completely exhausted, but he was smiling too. "The inspector cleared the pub to reopen."

He stared at Jar. "What? He was there today?"

Jar nodded. "He found one minor thing in the kitchen, and he made me promise I would take care of it. I can open any time I want."

"Holy shit—oh. Sorry, Ma. That's fantastic!" He grabbed Jar and hugged him, lifting his man right off his feet.

Kate was so happy, she was applauding. "Now we can celebrate tonight! I need to go tell Jim." She disappeared out to the deck.

He set Jar down and very chastely, because Ma was right there, kissed Jar's cheek. "This is amazing."

"The inspector showed up out of nowhere, and I wasn't ready for him. We had boxes and sh—stuff everywhere, and Nadine had just finished the last coat on the main floor. And —*boom*. He just walks in the door." Jar made an exasperated sound and shook his head. "And you know how it went last time. I thought I was done. I couldn't breathe the whole time he was there."

Scott huffed out a breath. "Well, damn."

"But he was in and out in less than half an hour. I couldn't believe it. He told me he was pleasantly surprised, and he replaced that evil orange sticker with a green one. Jesus, I'm so relieved. Kind of stunned, still, but I feel like I can breathe finally."

Jarlath was lit up and excited, talking a mile a minute, and Scott wanted to grab him and kiss the fuck out of him. That was going to have to wait a bit, but it was a plan now. As soon as he could.

Dad coughed gently behind him. "What is all the commotion, son?"

Scott stepped aside to make room for him in the conversation. "Oh, Dad. The inspector finally cleared O'Connolly's to open again."

Dad scowled at him. "Jarlath is perfectly capable of answering for himself."

"Oh." *Fine.* He swallowed down how much that hurt his feelings. It probably shouldn't have. Dad liked Jar, and "son" was an old man thing. Some old guys called everyone "son."

Dad didn't, but he told himself that didn't mean anything.

"Right. Sorry." Scott blew out a breath. "I'm going to get a beer. Anyone want one?"

Jar spoke up quickly, giving him an apologetic look. "Yeah. I would. Thanks, Scotty."

"Yep. I'll be right back."

He told himself to breathe. It was hard to know what Dad intended as a slight these days and what he just did without thinking or...or knowing any better. Scott ducked into the kitchen but was distracted by the deep dish of macaroni and cheese cooling on the stove. Nothing reminded him more of home than Ma's mac and cheese. Kate's potato salad was sitting on the counter next to a tray of stuffies wrapped up tight in foil and a big fruit salad. It might be fall, but Ma wasn't giving up summer yet.

He went to the fridge, pulled out two beers and opened them, already feeling better. Ma's kitchen was a warm place, a happy place. It was hard to hold a grudge with mac and cheese sitting on the stove.

"Hey, Scott? Can you grab the stuffies for Jim?"

"Oh, yeah. No problem. Here, Jar." He handed off Jar's beer with a nod and a smile. He wasn't mad, certainly not at Jarlath. Then he went back and carried the tray of stuffed quahogs out to Jim, who lined them up along one edge of the grill, right in the coals.

"Careful not to leave those too long."

"Oh, you're funny, Scott. I've learned my lesson. I put a timer on them now."

The first time Jim tried this trick, he'd left them in the coals so long that steam built up inside the foil, and they'd literally exploded. Thank God everyone had been a good distance from the grill so the story could be a funny one. That could have been ugly.

Jim started pulling the chicken off the grill as Kate set the table inside. It was just a little too cold once the sun went down to eat outside this time of year. The dining room was busy when he and Jim went inside—Noah was sitting in a high chair and Aiden in his booster seat; Jarlath was getting Dad settled at the head of the table; Ma was making sure all the napkins were just so and her favorite lighthouse salt and pepper shakers were on the table.

"Sit, everybody. Ma, sit." Kate made a "sit down" gesture with her hands. "I'm just going to get the fruit. Sit down, Scotty."

When Kate said sit, she meant everyone but Jim, and Jim knew it. He went right into the kitchen to see if he could help.

"Your mac smells amazing, Ma." Jarlath reached right for it but offered some to Dad first. "Can I give you a scoop, Dad?"

Dad nodded, looking grumpy. "Everybody is always serving me like I'm a child."

Ma clucked. "Oh, Ned. They're serving you because you've earned it."

"I'm going to serve Ma too, don't worry." Jar's tone was playful, trying to keep it light.

He was seated next to Jar and across from his nephews. Aiden was quietly driving a little wooden train across the table, which Kate took away and replaced with a bowl of mac and cheese. "Eat, buddy."

Aiden didn't miss a beat, just picked up his spoon and shoveled in a huge bite.

It was good to be home. He'd missed this. Neither of those boys had even been born when he left.

"So, Ma." Scott got Ma's attention, then looked at Jarlath, who nodded and took his hand. "I'm going to move in with Jarlath."

There was a collective gasp around the table and for a second Scott panicked, but it was quickly followed by smiles and encouragement.

"You guys. I'm so happy for you." Kate looked like she

might burst into tears. She even dabbed at the corner of her eyes with her napkin. "I'm sorry, I'm a sap. I'm just...I love you both so much."

"Thank you, Kate."

Jarlath looked down the table at Ma. "Don't you worry Ma, we'll be here a lot. We've talked about that, and we're not going to leave you lonely. We promise."

"Oh, don't you boys worry about me," Ma scoffed. "If I miss you, I'll just make some muffins, and Scotty will be back in a heartbeat."

Scott laughed. "Truth. Nothing but truth, Ma."

"I'm thrilled for all of us. My two favorite boys, and I get to keep them both." Ma sounded absolutely sincere, and Scott stood up so he could give her a kiss.

"I love you, Ma."

Dad was noticeably silent at his end of the table, but Scott let it go. It was totally possible Dad hadn't actually followed the conversation. If he had heard and had opinions, Scott didn't want to know about them anyway.

"So, next weekend?" Jim asked.

"Hopefully. I'm going to take stuff over little by little. I don't have much. I'm expecting my things from San Francisco soon, but there's not much of that either."

He'd sent a bunch of boxes and some furniture as freight with a moving company, and it would be a couple of weeks yet before it arrived. They'd stored it, waiting for a truck heading east, and his crate hadn't even left the Bay Area until a few days ago.

"Where are you going to keep your bike?"

"Hm. Well, here for now." He hadn't thought about that. Maybe he'd need to get a car.

Jar held a finger up while he finished chewing and said, "We'll build a garage."

Scott looked at him. "Yeah?"

"Yeah. I already thought about it. Dad's old shed is sturdy but kind of ugly, and I have lots of power tools I'll need a place for anyway. We can tear that down, extend the driveway, and build a garage where the shed is now."

He couldn't help smiling as he looked at Jim again. "We're building a garage."

Laughter went around the table.

"What is this? Peas? You know I hate peas."

"I know, Ned, but the kids love them. There's corn, Kate cut some off the cob for you."

"Why would you serve peas when you know I hate them?"

"Dad."

"Don't 'Dad' me!" Dad shouted, dropping his fork on the table. "Why does everyone talk around me like I'm not sitting right here?"

"Ned, no one is talking about you."

"Jim is out there cooking on my grill, you serve food you know I won't eat, and Scott's leaving again."

"I'm not leaving, Dad."

"You're moving, aren't you?"

"Well, yes, but only—"

"Did you not promise me you would look after your mother? You promised, Scotty. I'm not the man I used to be and you—" Dad tried for a deep breath but it was rough and made him cough. Ma took his hand, but he shook her off. "Don't touch me!"

"Dad." Scott stood and moved down the table. "I'm staying close like I promised. I'm not leaving town, I'm just moving in with Jar over in Davisville. That's all."

Kate got up and swept the kids out of the room, and Jim

followed her with their plates. He watched Ma sink farther into her chair.

"Dad?"

Dad looked at him helplessly, his heart sank too. This man was old and confused, his eyes were dull. Not Dad. Not anyone. "Are we still having dinner?"

"Sure Dad. Sure. Have some corn."

Dad turned back to his meal and started eating.

Jim returned to the table, but he made excuses for Kate, who was staying with the boys in the other room while they watched TV and finished their dinners. He and Jar sat again, too. The table was quiet as they ate, Dad was given a piece of pie that he took two bites of, and the rest of them enjoyed Ma's pie while Jim took Dad to the home.

He had a terrible feeling this could be the last family dinner they would have.

"I'm sorry about the peas," Ma said with a sigh as she got up from the table.

"Oh, Ma." Scott went to her, thinking he'd get her to her chair, but she wanted to go right to her bedroom.

"I don't know what promises you made to your father, Scotty, but I am just fine."

"I know you are, Ma. I only promised him I wouldn't go back to San Francisco, and I'm not. He's worried about you, he doesn't want you to be alone, that's all."

Ma sighed again and nodded.

"He loves you, Ma. That's what it's about. He wants you to be okay."

She stopped and rested a hand on his chest. "He loves you too, you know. Despite the way he talks. He loves you very much."

"I know." He wasn't sure about "very much," but he and Dad had an understanding, and they loved each other.

"Turn your back and let your old mother get her nightgown on."

"Yes, Ma." He turned so he couldn't see. "Your pie was delicious. You know how much I love your pies."

"Thank you." There was a pause, and he could hear her shuffling around. "You see why he couldn't live here anymore. I feel so guilty but I just couldn't...manage it."

"I understand, Ma. And don't feel guilty. I think he actually understands. We all do. This is really hard, and there's no easy answer."

"I suppose that's true. Still, I wish I hadn't had to send him there. You may turn around now."

Scott went right to his mother and hugged her. "It's okay, Ma. We all love you."

"That much I do know, Scotty. You're a good boy. It was a good night, wasn't it? Jar's news about the pub...and I couldn't be happier for the two of you, it's just wonderful to see you together."

"It was a great night. Thanks, Ma." He folded her blankets back for her. "You know, I think...I mean, I don't think, I *know* I love him."

Ma smiled as she got into bed. "He loves you too. I can see it. I know love."

He believed that; Ma was love in all its forms. "You all set here?"

"Oh, yes. I'm just going to read for a bit."

"Okay. We'll clean up, there are lots of us." He'd scrub the grill for Jim, Kate and Jar could do the dishes, and they'd all be done in no time. He lingered in the doorway to the bedroom for another second. "Thank you for having all of us."

"Let's do it again soon." She smiled at him, and despite everything, he knew she meant it.

"Good night, Ma."

"Good night, son."

He closed her door quietly and turned around, nearly tripping over Aiden. "Is Grandma asleep?"

"She will be any minute." He lifted Aiden up into his arms. "Where's Mommy?"

"Washing dishes. Did Grandpa go home mad?"

Oh, boy. "No, Grandpa went home tired. You know how sometimes you get grumpy when you're tired?"

Aiden nodded. "Yeah."

"Well, that's what happened. Grandpa got grumpy. He'll be fine. He loves everybody very much."

"Okay. I hope he sleeps good." Aiden smiled and wiggled to get down.

"He will. What did you think of Grandma's pie?"

"Yummy!"

"The best pie on Cape Cod, right?"

"Right!" Aiden turned his head as something Scott didn't recognize came on TV, and then he ran off. Conversation over. He thought it had gone pretty well.

Ma was right, it had been a good night.

25

"Hey, Boss? Can you come out to the bar a second?"

Jarlath looked up from his laptop at Ezra. It wasn't like he was getting any work done. "Sure. Everything okay? We open in like twenty minutes."

"Yeah, it's all good. We're ready. I just want to show you something."

"Okay." He was curious now. He followed Ezra out to the bar, to find everyone—literally everyone that was on tonight —huddled around the bar. "Whoa. Hey everybody. What's going on?"

"Well," Nadine stepped up next to him and steered him into the middle of the dance floor. "We are all so grateful for how hard you worked to keep giving us even a small paycheck while the pub was closed, and we know how difficult these last couple of months have been for you."

"What did you folks do?" he joked.

"Well, Ezra knew how bummed out you were about your dad's desk."

Uh-oh. "His desk...?"

Nadine nodded. "Ezra, tell him what you did."

Jarlath watched as Ezra walked toward the front entrance, and that was when he saw something hanging over the door with a cloth over it.

"I took the top of the desk home and some of the hardware. The rest of the desk was pretty much toast from sitting in the water, but the top was dry as a bone. Anyway, I figured out what I wanted to do with it, I cut it down to a good size and started carving."

"Carving?"

Ezra pulled the cloth down and he stared as people applauded. "Oh, my God. Ezra..." He went to it and reached up, touching the large plaque that was now hung over the door. It read, "Sean O'Connolly was here," and there were brass drawer handles on either end as decoration. "This is amazing." He looked at Ezra, not bothering to hide that he was tearing up. "Thank you so much."

"You like it?"

"Ezra, I love it. It's perfect, and so thoughtful and...Dad's *desk*. I can't believe it." He went to shake Ezra's hand but pulled his bartender and closest friend into a hug instead. "Really, this means a lot. I'm so happy. It's perfect."

"I couldn't just watch that old desk go away, and I knew you weren't in a state of mind to be thinking creatively, so I just—"

"It's fantastic. Honestly. I'm just...blown away. Hey! Everyone gets a round on me when we close tonight. Anything you want." They were opening for Friday happy hour, so they were in for a long night. He couldn't wait. "Is everyone ready to do Sean O'Connolly proud?"

"Yes!" There was clapping and cheering, and he loved all the smiles.

"Okay, then. Nadine? Ready?"

"I am!"

"Ezra? Benny?"

"You know it. But...can I just ask....What's with the inflatable lobster?" Benny poked at the bright-red lobster he'd hung on the back mirror. He'd kind of been hoping no one would notice.

"Scott won that for me at the fundraiser." *There.* He'd kept his promise.

Everyone in the room said "aww" all at once and made him blush.

Dammit.

He had to laugh, though.

"Where is Scott, by the way?"

"He's bringing Mrs. Borden. She wanted to celebrate with some fried clams."

"No way."

Jarlath shrugged. "Just be polite, people, she'll only be here a little while. Oh, and Nadine?"

"I will keep her booth empty."

"Teamwork makes the dream work." Jarlath couldn't stop smiling. "I'm opening the doors!" The rest of his staff cheered and scattered to the kitchen or the bar or the hostess stand.

He unlocked the door and opened it to more cheering. There had to be thirty people lined up along the sidewalk, waiting to get in. And the first two in line?

Jim and Kate.

"Hey! There's a line...how are you here? Who has the kids?"

"There's this magical thing called a babysitter. Are you going to let us in?"

Jarlath chuckled and stepped out of the way. "Oh. Sorry!"

Nadine started seating people, and Ezra had a nearly full

bar in less than half an hour. He should've gone to check on the kitchen or check the stock behind the bar, but instead he stood in the doorway, welcoming people as they came in, and looking around at the dream he almost lost. People were eating, drinking, laughing...just like every Friday night happy hour.

Like the fucking hurricane had never happened.

"Look who's here!" Scott had Ma on his arm and they were just reaching the doorway.

"Hey, Ma! Nadine has your booth for you."

"Does she? What a sweetheart. Oh my, it's busy, Jarlath."

He kissed her cheek and escorted them to the booth. "It's fantastic, Ma. It's amazing."

"You must be so proud." She sat. "I hope you have your fried clams on the menu."

"We do. Nadine will put the order in."

"Hi, Mrs. Borden. Did you want something to drink?"

Iced tea. Ezra had made a pitcher for her and it was behind the bar.

Ma smiled. "Do you have iced tea, dear?"

"We do. Scott?"

Scott looked surprised. "Oh, uh. I'll have the fish and chips and a Fiddlehead IPA, please."

"Sounds good." Nadine left, and Jarlath slid into the seat beside Scott.

"I didn't expect so many people so early. We might get slammed later." He looked at Scott.

"I'm coming back after I take Ma home, if you need help..."

"That would be great. I'm going to need help with something. I can pretty much guarantee it. Plus, I would just love to have you here."

"Well, I do need a job."

"Oh. You have a job. We'll figure out what it is, but you work here now."

"Listening to you boys making plans makes me so happy." Ma reached out and touched both of them, giving each a hand squeeze.

"Iced tea and a Fiddlehead."

Ma started stirring her tea right away. "Thank you, dear."

Nadine touched his shoulder. "Jarlath, it's not an emergency, but they had a question in the kitchen."

"Right. No problem." He slid out of the booth. "Gotta work, Ma. I'll come and check on you in a bit."

"Don't you worry, Scotty will take good care of me." She smiled. "Congratulations."

"Thanks, Ma." Jarlath took off for the kitchen, beaming, and hoping whatever was going on there wouldn't ruin his mojo.

————

"Jarlath really did a nice job fixing this place up, Scotty. It looks brand new. Shinier than it was before the flood." Ma was craning her neck and looking at everything as if she'd never seen the place.

Scott agreed, it was gorgeous. "He worked hard. Everyone did."

"You too."

Scott shrugged. "Yeah, I did. I wanted to, though, it wasn't—it never felt like work, you know? It meant so much to Jar, and I felt like I was doing something that mattered."

One of the food runners arrived with Nadine on his heels. "The clams are for Mrs. Borden," she told him. "Thanks, Philip."

"Enjoy, everybody." Philip hurried off.

"Oh, I'm so excited. These smell so good. It's been forever since I've had fried clams."

They both knew Ma was going to have to go easy on her stomach, but she never ate that much in one sitting anymore anyway.

"This looks perfect." He lifted a hunk of fried fish out of the little basket lined with newspaper, dipped it into the side of malt vinegar, and took a bite. The salty tang of the vinegar, the crunchy fried bits, and the smooth taste of the fish were perfect. "Mmm. So good."

Ma did a little chair dance as she chewed her clams, and he had to smile. She was so damn cute. "Good, Ma?"

"My favorite."

"Scotty! We've been waiting for you two to get here."

"Hey, Jim, Kate. Sit down. We just got our dinner." Jim and Kate slid into the booth, Kate next to him and Jim next to Ma.

Kate took his arm and smiled at him. "Everything looks so good, and people seem so happy."

"Right? I think folks missed the place. That's so cool."

"So when is your move final?"

"Tomorrow. I just need to pick up a couple more things this weekend. Almost everything is moved already. We're going to start on the new garage on Monday when the pub is closed." He and Jar had been looking at styles and drawing plans, and he was pretty sure they could do it all themselves. It would take some time, but they'd figure it out.

"You know you can use my car any time, Scotty. I hardly ever drive it anymore."

He nodded. "Thanks, Ma. I would love to keep up our food shopping trips."

"It's a date." She smiled and touched his hand. "Friday mornings."

"Fridays. I'm there."

Kate squeezed his arm. "So?"

He blinked at her. "So...what?"

She sighed, exasperated. "When are you going to do it?"

He squinted at Ma. "Someone's been gossiping?"

Ma rolled her eyes. "Telling family is not gossiping. I was just so excited, and it was so sweet that you asked me first. I'm not even Jarlath's mother."

"Well, you're the closest he has."

Jim leaned over the table. "Wait, what am I missing here?"

"Can I tell him, Scotty? Hm?"

He snorted. "Yes, Kate. Go ahead."

"Scotty is going to ask Jarlath to marry him tonight."

"Maybe. Maybe tonight. Maybe...tomorrow. Or soon."

"Tonight, Scotty. It'll be perfect. A night to remember."

"He's going to remember today anyway, trust me."

"Scotty." Jim laughed and leaned back in his seat, looking smug. "Trust me, when it comes to proposals, go with what the women say."

He rolled his eyes. He wanted to do it tonight, but if anything was off—if Jar was too tired, or the night turned out to be stressful—he wasn't going to. "To be honest you guys, I'm not even sure he's going to say yes. I just need it to be...perfect."

"Son." Ma touched his hand and looked him right in the eyes, the green in hers as bright as ever. "Don't overthink it."

Now that was good advice. "You know me, huh, Ma?"

"I raised you, Scotty. Don't let the right moment slip past you because you're waiting for something more perfect."

Jim shrugged. "I'm telling you, Scott, the ladies know."

"Ha." Kate snorted. "Says the man who carried my ring around in his pocket for a month."

"Two, actually." Ma patted Jim's arm.

"Ma! You snitch!"

He and Ma laughed, and Kate kissed Jim in consolation. "It's okay, baby, I'd have said yes anytime."

"I am so full," Ma said, leaning back in the booth. "That was wonderful."

"You're done? Do you mind?" Jim slid her plate over and popped a couple of pieces into his mouth.

"Nothing goes to waste with Jim around." Kate reached for Scott's fries and helped herself. "He's always stealing other people's food."

"Imagine that?"

"You guys! Look at all of you. Thank you all for coming, really. It means a lot." Jarlath dragged a chair over and sat at the end of the table.

"Oh, hey. We were just getting ready to take Ma home, Jar." Jim wiped his fingers on a napkin.

Scott blinked. Wasn't he supposed to be...? "Are you sure? I can take her home."

"Yeah. You stay and hang out. We have to get back to the sitter and everything." Kate slid out of the booth and Jar stood up again.

"I'm so excited you were here. We're going to be busy tonight, I think."

"All the more reason for me to get home. You know how I am when things get loud." Jim helped Ma up and she held her arms out for Jar. "Congratulations. I know you're going to have a successful night."

"Thanks, Ma. I think so too. It's amazing." Jarlath gave her a big hug and they all walked toward the door.

"You deserve it."

"Oh! Did you guys see my new sign? Ezra made it from Dad's desk."

Scott knew about it, but he hadn't gotten a good look at it yet. "Right! He told me he was going to put it up today. It looks amazing."

"It's the best gift...I got all emotional earlier. Ugh. But it's...I love it."

Scott circled an arm around Jar's shoulders, fingers curling over strong muscle, and Jar leaned into him while everyone admired the plaque.

"This place means a lot to a lot of people." Ma kissed Jar's cheek, then his. "Remember what I told you."

"Yes, Ma."

"Good night, everyone." They all said their good-byes and Jim helped Ma out the door.

"Can you sit a minute? The fish and chips are amazing. Come have a bite."

"For a minute, okay."

They went back to the booth and Scott pushed his basket into the middle of the table. "Everything going well?"

"Yes. Things are fine. Ezra and Benny might need your help later. Are you in?"

"I'm in. Yes. I'm totally in." He wanted to help, wanted to be part of Jarlath's night. Of Jarlath's everything.

"I'll have Benny barback; he set everything up for me today, so he knows where everything is. Once he trains you, you all can trade off."

"Does that mean I'm hired?"

"Are you still looking for a job?"

"Apparently not. I have one." He leaned over the booth and gave Jar a kiss. "Thank you."

"And thank you." Jar took a piece of fish out of the basket. "A bite, and then we have to go be useful."

"Sure. I can fire up the jukebox. Is that useful enough?" He winked at Jar.

"It's a tough job, but someone's got to do it." Jar took a big bite of the fish and hummed happily. "It's like finally being home."

He gave Jar a teasing grin. "So, I should move in here tomorrow?"

"Ha. No." Jar waggled his eyebrows. "There's no bed here."

"Excellent point. I do enjoy your bed." A lot. Especially with Jar in it.

"Soon to be our bed."

"Oh, I like the sound of that." Not that he hadn't spent nearly every night there this week. He just hadn't officially made the move yet.

"Good." Jar stood, leaned across the table, and kissed him. "Ready, set, work."

"You know it, Boss."

26

"Limes." Benny took the nearly empty tub away and sat a fresh, full one down where it had been.

"You rock, Benny." Ezra took one right that second, popped it on the rim of a margarita, and handed it to a lady Scott didn't recognize but had to be a regular. "One refreshing margarita, Nan. Hang on, I've got Timmy's Guinness too." Ezra poured it perfectly, leaving a nice white head at the top. "Here you go. On your tab?"

"Yes, please. Thanks, Ezra." She left a few bucks on the bar, and Ezra swept them into the tip jar.

"Hey! Is that Scotty? Are you back behind the bar now?" The salty accent was thick, very old Cape Cod, and unmistakably related to him. Scotty looked up and smiled.

"Hey, Uncle Mark. Just making myself useful. What can I get you?"

"I'm here with Eddie and his wife. Have you met Linda? She's a riot."

Uncle Mark would talk forever and never order. "Not yet, no. Does she drink beer?" He was pretty proud of that prompt.

"Aw, no. She'll have one of those Stella spritzers."

Score. "Okay, and you and Eddie?"

"You got Whale's Tail?"

Scott pointed to the tap handle with the blue whale's tail on it and Mark laughed. "Two pints?"

"Sounds good."

He poured them while Uncle Mark talked and talked, answering all of his own questions as usual. Scott grabbed a spritzer and set everything on the bar. "Two pints of Whale's Tail Pale Ale." Scott played with the words, enjoying the rhyme. "Where are you guys? You need me to bring the spritzer over?"

"Thanks. I'll just—"

"Hey, Scotty!" Eddie stepped up behind his dad and took his beer. "Is that for Linda?"

"Yep." He reached up and pulled down a wineglass to go with the spritzer. "There you go. Are you guys running a tab?"

"Yeah, for sure," Eddie replied. "Dad's just here for one, but Linda and I are going to dance."

"Nice."

"Scotty's tending bar again," Mark said, pointing to him.

"Looks like it. Hey. So, you're staying in town?"

He nodded. "Home for good."

"He and Jarlath are a thing now." Uncle Mark nodded like he knew everything there was to know, and Scott tried not to snort.

"Yeah? Cool. Congrats. So, Scott," Eddie went on, glossing right over Scott's news with an agenda of his own. "I was just thinking—you used to play football here in high school, right?"

He loved football. He'd even played in a casual rec league in San Francisco. He was a fan, and he was probably going to drive Jarlath bananas. "I did. Varsity quarterback." Okay, so that was a little braggy, but he didn't get to say it often.

"Yeah, I thought so. You still play?" Eddie started digging around in his pockets and pulled out a phone.

"I'd like to. I played some rec out west, is there a club here?"

"Yeah, man. You wanna play? I'm on it, I'll get you in. Give me your number."

Scott took Eddie's phone and made a contact for himself. "Sounds like fun."

"It's a good group. The league is great, we're serious about practices and workouts, but it's that friendly and fun kind of competitive, you know? We always need more players. I'll call you."

"Awesome. Thanks." Football. Cool. "Tell Linda that her spritzer is on me. Looking forward to meeting her." Eddie looked exactly like Uncle Mark but was definitely more chill, and Scott was impressed at how he'd figured out a way to wrestle the conversation away from his dad.

Eddie smiled. "Can't wait to hang out. Thanks. Come on, Dad."

Uncle Mark raised his glass in salute. "Good beer," he said and turned to follow Eddie.

The lights dimmed and shifted and Scott looked at his watch. Nine o'clock. "Mood lighting." He remembered this. "I got the jukebox!"

"Right on," Ezra laughed and called after him.

He ducked out from behind the bar and went right for it, starting out the night with some Bob Seger. Sure, it was an oldie. But who didn't want to dance when "Old Time Rock and Roll" came on?

Right. Everyone knew it, and sure enough, the dance floor was filling up by the time the first chorus hit.

Even Jarlath showed up, dancing toward him and grinning broadly. "Good choice," he shouted over the guitars and danced right into his arms.

"Hey, there." He rocked Jar awkwardly for a second, startled and a little stupid with the scent of Jar's cologne. He finally snapped out of it and tried to remember his high school dance days. He gave Jar a spin, figured out his lead, and danced Jarlath into the crowd.

Now, he thought. *Now would be a good time. Right after this dance.* But there were too many people around, and it was too loud, and the shift was nowhere near over. They had work to do still. So this wasn't his moment, but man, he was feeling it.

The song ended and someone had already chosen the next one. The night was off to a great start. "Thanks for the dance."

"That was the best dance ever." Jarlath was all pink-cheeked and smiling.

"I think it was our first dance ever." He'd never had the courage to try it in high school—he'd only ever danced with the girls.

"Let's make that a tradition." Jar pulled him toward the bar. "That song. First of the night, every weekend."

"You got it." He loved that idea. A new tradition. Their tradition.

"We can follow it with George Thorogood."

"Oh, I took that one out of rotation after you came in that night."

"What?" Scott laughed.

Ezra gave him a wave. He didn't look panicked, but the music had made the bar popular.

"Oops. Looks like I need to work."

"Well, hurry up, before the boss finds out you were dancing." Jar squeezed his hand and headed for his office, and Scott got his dancing butt back behind the bar.

The rest of the night went by quickly. One minute it was nine and the next it was last call. It wasn't a club scene kind of bar, so by last call most people had cleared out. There was one couple on the dance floor swaying to their own music, and he and Benny were cleaning up behind the bar while Ezra chatted up a young, sweet, and very drunk group of friends while they waited for their Uber.

He wandered over at exactly twelve fifty-five, shut down the jukebox, and turned on the work lights. The pub emptied out without any hassle in minutes.

"So weird after living in San Francisco. Bars there don't close until two, so this feels early."

"The Cape is early. Always has been. Did you spend a lot of time closing down bars out there?" Ezra shot him a knowing look.

"On the weekends, more often than not." He'd been a bit of a partier out there. He'd worked his ass off all week and danced out the stress every weekend.

"That's a wrap, guys." Nadine leaned on the bar, looking tired but happy. "That felt good, didn't it?"

Ezra nodded. "It did. You want Benny to mop?"

"That would be great. I'll just get the chairs up. Lucy can help." Nadine tapped the bar and got to work.

"How are we doing? Getting cleaned up?" Jarlath appeared again, this time wearing an apron and looking a little disheveled.

"Kitchen?" he asked.

"Oh, yeah." Jar looked down at the apron like he'd forgotten it and pulled it off. "They got a little weeded for a bit, so I jumped in. That was hours ago, though." Jar added his apron to the pile of bar towels.

They all worked for the next half hour, getting the pub back to rights. He put all the towels and aprons in the washer, Jar got through the receipts, Ezra and Nadine made the front of house shipshape. The kitchen had been done for ages, they shut down at ten. It was nearly two when they all headed out.

Jar looked around the pub and shut the lights off, then locked the door behind him. "Good night, everyone. Thank you and see you tomorrow." Scott didn't miss Jar's sigh of relief. "We did it."

He tucked an arm over Jar and pulled him in. "We did. It was a seriously smooth reopening, Jar. Congratulations."

"Thank you. We smell like hell, though."

Scott laughed. "Welcome to bartending. You ready to go?"

"You have Ma's car. Are you following me or going—"

"I'm following you." That was certain. He had a ring burning a hole in his pocket.

He got a warm smile. "Good. Let's go home."

He got into the car and followed Jar out of the parking lot. "Jar," he said out loud, practicing. "Jarlath? Jar." Jesus, he had no idea what he was going to say. He thought it would just come to him. Shouldn't it just...be there? Maybe he shouldn't propose if the right words weren't there. Maybe this was a mistake.

Maybe.

Maybe he was overthinking like Ma said.

But seriously, what was he doing? He hadn't said "I love you" to anyone but Ma and Kate in...well, maybe ever. He hadn't even said it to Jar yet. He knew, he hoped they both knew, but he hadn't actually said it.

So that was the answer. "Okay. I can say that, right? Jar. This has been a long, winding road for us, but I'm where I belong finally, and...uh. And what? And I want to stay for good. I want to...I want you to be my forever. Oh. That's good. And I love you. I love you and I want you to be my forever."

Yeah. Okay. That's good. Then the "will you marry me" thing and the ring and...yeah.

"Okay, Scott. You've got this."

And not a minute too soon. He followed as Jar turned down his street, and they both parked out front. He put Ma's car where the garage would eventually be, and Jarlath waited for him by the front door.

"Guess what?" Jar watched him as he got closer, eyes roaming over him in a hungry way.

"Yes?" His curiosity made him grin and his skin tingle.

"It's Saturday now, and that means, you officially live here." Jar went up on his toes and kissed him gently. "Welcome home."

"Thank you." Oh, now. Right now. This was great timing. His heart was pounding and he stuck his hand into his pocket, going for the ring before he lost his nerve. "Jar, I—"

"Hang on." Jar held one hand up, stopping his. "Before we go in...here." Jarlath dangled a New England Patriots keychain in front of his eyes with a key to the house on it.

And a ring.

He stared at it, watched the silver catch the moonlight, and his palms started to sweat. His heart tried to beat right out of his chest. "Oh, my God."

Jar touched his cheek and ran slightly shaking fingers along his jaw. "I'm really glad you agreed to move in with me. Not that leaving your childhood bedroom and twin bed was much of a hardship, I guess, but it means a lot to me. More than I have words for."

Scott nodded. He knew exactly how hard the words were. He knew he should say something, but he was so stunned. Had they really both—

"I'm sorry your company folded, and that dream didn't work out for you, I truly am. But I am so happy you came back home, and I need you to know how much I want you. You make everything better. Easier. And I want to give you every reason to stay. With me. I love you, Scott." Jar opened the clasp on the key ring, removed the heavy-looking, smooth, silver ring, then went down on one knee.

Don't overthink it.

This was perfect fucking timing.

He pulled out Jarlath's ring and dropped to one knee too. "Scott?"

"Jar." He opened the ring box, which contained a remarkably similar heavy, silver ring, and held it out. "I love you. I'm staying here with you. I want you to be my forever."

"Oh, my God. Scott."

"I know. But I'm going to say it first. Will you marry me?"

Jarlath's smile was bright and happy. "Yes, I will. Will you marry me?"

"Yes. It wouldn't take a ring to keep me here, but I will marry you."

"This is crazy."

"I love that we just did this. It's so—"

"Us." Jar interrupted.

"So totally us." They stared into each other's eyes for a moment; then Scott put the ring on Jar's finger and kissed him. Jar returned the gesture with his ring and pressed the key into his hand as they stood.

"You get the door."

He smiled. "Okay." He put his new key in the lock and turned it. "The Patriots key ring is a nice touch."

"I was buttering you up."

"I don't need buttering up." Scott went inside and closed the door. "I need a shower, though." He dropped his car keys and his new house key on the hall table.

"Mmm. You do. So do I." Jar put a hand on his ass and steered him toward the bedroom, not bothering to turn on any lights. The moon lit the bedroom as it always did, and they undressed each other there, hands roaming and teasing as their clothing fell to the floor.

They'd been so concerned about words earlier, and now they didn't need any. The water was hot and rained down as they cleaned up, indulging in every opportunity to touch and tease. Jar's fingers spread over his shoulders as he faced the spray and smoothed down his back to his ass. Hot lips pressed into his shoulders, and a hand slipped over his hip and pushed down into the curls at the base of his cock.

He turned around and returned the touch, sliding his fingers along Jar's perfect, long cock, the hot, silky length calling to him, begging him to stroke and satisfy. Jar groaned and leaned against the wall of the shower, and damned if he didn't look like a fucking model all sexy and wet, lips parted, panting lightly.

Jar wasn't a model, though, he was Scott's fucking fiancé, *thank you*, and Scott intended to treat him like one. He kissed Jar hard, tasting the depths of Jar's throat with his tongue and working that cock through his fingers. Jar moaned and writhed, hands digging into his skin, holding on.

Yeah, that was what he wanted. He was going to drive Jar out of his mind.

He reached back and shut the water off and he and Jar

stepped out of the shower, dripping everywhere. Jar grabbed a towel and sort of dried off with it, but without breaking the kiss, he could only do so good a job. Scott grabbed a towel too and herded Jar into the bedroom, where he tossed it onto the bed and crowded Jar until he landed on top of it.

There.

"Scott. Fuck."

He nodded and tossed Jar the lube before dealing with his condom, but he didn't want to wait. He leaned over Jar and watched his fiancé's face as Jar lubed himself a little, knees hauled up to his chest.

"Ready?"

"I want you."

"Uh-huh. But are you ready?"

"Yeah. Yes. Fuck, Scott." Jar tossed the lube somewhere, and he didn't hesitate to line up and sink in—carefully, but purposefully—inch by inch, and watching Jar's face go from tight to wide-eyed to openmouthed, shameless need. "More. Fuck, baby. More."

More he had.

Scott got one knee up on the bed and leaned into it, bending Jar and exposing that perfect ass, giving Jar his weight along with his full length. Jar cried out, trying to arch or buck or roll, but Scott had him pretty well pinned and Jar finally relaxed, babbling his name and a million other things.

"Scott. So good. More, please. Oh, Jesus, Scott. There... right there..."

Things like that. Things that made his balls ache and his head swim. Things that spoke to the man that had wanted Jarlath for years, even three thousand miles away, and had regretted not being here, at home, to do just exactly this.

He'd never gotten over Jarlath, and now, he swore he never would.

"Scott!" Jar raked in a breath and arched hard, hips finding some way, any way to move. "Please. So...oh, God."

"Yeah...yes. Come on, Jar." He caught Jar's straining cock in his hand, working it across his palm as he thrust in deep.

"Yes! Scott..." The sound Jarlath made was long and low, a release, a deep, satisfying orgasm that Scott watched with wonder.

Until Jar went tight around his cock, stealing his breath and making his eyes cross. "Fuck!"

"Do it. Come on, baby. You want it." Jesus, Jar's voice was blown. So fucking hot.

"Yes. Fuck, yes. Jar..." A few erratic, clumsy thrusts later and he shot so hard his ears rang and his vision went dark for a second.

They were both breathless, the room filled with panting and little moans and grunts as Scott slipped free, tossed the condom in the wastebasket, and climbed onto the bed, where he could pull Jarlath into his arms.

"Mmm." Jar rested against him heavily, one hand sliding over his abs. "That was amazing."

"Mhm," he agreed.

"I love that you make me feel so wanted."

"You are wanted." He turned his head and kissed Jar's temple. "You're...everything I need. Really. Everything."

"Except beer."

"Except beer. But no one is beer. Those are some big shoes to fill." He chuckled.

"I love you, Scott. I've been worried—I was afraid to say it."

He nodded, because he'd known. For a while. "I love you too. Don't ever be afraid to say it."

"I won't be now, I'm putting a ring on it."

"No, *I'm* putting a ring on it."

They both cracked up, sex-blown voices filling the room.

27

Scotty wore a suit like no one Jarlath had ever seen. Something about Scott's broad shoulders and trim waist made a suit jacket look so hot on him, as if he were born to wear one. He knew this was their wedding and he should be paying much closer attention to what the officiant was saying but honestly, he couldn't take his eyes off his man.

His man. Soon to be his husband. The man that had consistently showed up, stood up, held him up...whatever he'd needed since the second they'd laid eyes on each other at the end of last summer.

And this was how they'd decided to kick off the next one. A spring wedding on the beach, with a view of O'Connolly's in the background.

"Do you..."

Oh, shit. Okay, this part he had to pay attention to.

Scott looked into his eyes, and *damn*...first the suit, and now those gorgeous bright-blue eyes, *blue like the summer sky*, threatened to distract him from his own declarations. He was so fucking in love it hurt, and he wanted nothing more than to make this official, to give Scott back as much as Scott had already given him. He wanted to make promises to Scott he intended to keep until his dying day. Beyond it if he could.

"I do," Scott answered, so freely giving him everything.

Oops. Pay attention, Jarlath.

"And do you, Jarlath Sean O'Connolly, take Scott Edward Borden to be your lawfully wedded husband? To live your life openly, to stand beside him in sickness and in health, in joy and in sorrow, in hardship and ease, to love and to cherish forever?"

"I do." He squeezed Scott's hands. "I do, Scott. I love you so much."

Scott smiled at him warmly. "I love you too. But shh. He still has to say the important part."

Jarlath blushed, hearing all the giggles from the front couple of rows.

"Right." He looked at their officiant, but he couldn't help his smile. "Sorry."

"Don't be. Are you ready?"

"Yes." Jarlath chuckled. "I'm so ready."

"Gentlemen. I now pronounce you husbands together. You may—"

Oh, he had this part.

He leaned in and Scott met him halfway, and they kissed as everyone exploded into applause.

On the edge of the beach, a bagpiper began to play a bright and energetic exit march. Scott took his hand, held on tight, and walked him up the temporary little wooden boardwalk they'd put down so Ma didn't have to walk in the sand and Dad's wheelchair could make it down to the front row. They walked toward the piper, who then turned and led them to the entrance of The Wharf, where a whole line of pipers on one side and drummers on the other created a path.

"This is amazing," Jar shouted over the pipes.

Scotty nodded, smiling wider than Jarlath had ever seen. "I love this."

They walked down the line between the pipers and drummers and into the reception hall, followed by their guests, all of whom they greeted on the way in.

It was a small group but a lively one. There was a special head table for close family, and Ma and Dad were already seated by the time they were done at the door.

"My boys. You both look so handsome," Ma said, smiling as they came over to kiss her cheek.

"You do clean up nicely, both of you. Well, Scotty I would expect, he got his good looks from me." Dad grinned and chuckled at his own joke.

Jarlath stared at him.

"That was funny, Dad." Scott patted Dad on the shoulder.

It was funny. And lucid. Like Dad was totally in there right now.

"Nonsense, Ned. Both of our children got their good looks from me." Ma was happy, smiling.

"Of course, dear." Dad winked at her and she actually blushed.

That was amazing. Scott's dad was totally here for their wedding.

"Hey, there, husbands." Kate crossed the dance floor to them with Jim right behind her.

"Hey, there, sister of the groom."

"Grooms," she corrected. "I've officially got two brothers now."

"You look beautiful, Kate. And Jim, so handsome, I don't think I've ever seen you in a suit."

"Probably not, and don't get used to it." Jim shook his head. "I hate ties. I only wear them for weddings and funerals."

Jarlath leaned in and whispered, "Ties were optional for guests."

Kate snorted. "Oh, hell no. I get a chance to see my man in a suit and tie, and neither of you is taking that from me."

Even Dad laughed at that one.

"Would you like to get some food, Ma? It's a buffet." They'd cut some corners so they could afford the bagpipes.

"Oh, I do love a buffet."

Jarlath helped her up. "We'll be right back...husband."

"I'll be right here, husband," Scott replied, a little of that teenage kid he remembered smiling back at him.

Man, they were a couple of goons.

————

ALL SCOTT WANTED to do was dance with his husband. The ceremony was great, the buffet was spectacular, all their friends were dressed up and having fun, but he'd been eyeballing the empty dance floor for half an hour.

It was time to get the party started.

Scott set his drink down and got up from the table, casually wandering over to introduce himself to the DJ.

"Hey, there."

"Oh. Hi, Scott. Congratulations. Can I help you?"

Smart man, remembering the name of the guy that was going to write you a check at the end of the night. "Yes. I definitely need your help. I need music. I want to dance with my husband."

The DJ smiled at him. "I can do that. Like, now? I'm ready."

"Yes, now, please. What's your name?"

"Ian."

"Thank you, Ian." He gave Ian a nod and headed back to his husband.

As the music started, Jarlath looked up from his seat with a smile brighter than the summer sun. Patti Page was singing, and Ma's face lit up too.

"Oh. Oh, Ned, do you hear?"

Scott held out a hand. "May I have this dance?"

Jarlath took Scott's hand and they stepped onto the dance floor, where Scott pulled his husband into his arms for their first dance as a married couple.

"This is so perfect." Jar rested his head on Scott's shoulder.

"It is." He could just stay right here all night, no matter what music was playing, holding Jar in his arms and just breathing his husband in.

They did have other things planned, though.

They'd picked this song for themselves, because it was sentimental and had meaning for them both, but also because it reminded them of Ma, and they knew how happy it would make her.

Jim hopped up about halfway through the song as they'd planned. He took Ma's arm as Kate rolled Dad's wheelchair out to join Scott and Jarlath on the dancefloor. Ma looked shocked at first, but happy, and she did the best she could to dance with Dad, holding hands and moving with the music like it was the most natural thing in the world.

"Look, Jar." He turned them so they could both watch.

"Look at her face."

"Look at Dad's." Scott was stunned. Dad was smiling and moving his arms with her, both of them caught up in each other's eyes. It was incredible. More than he could have hoped for.

He didn't know how many lucid days Dad had left, but he was grateful for this one.

Their first dance ended with applause and when the next song started, so did the party.

"Bob Seger!" Jarlath laughed and spun him around. "So perfect."

EPILOGUE

"Whoa. Scott? Hey, Scott?"

Oh, boy. That was the new bartender. He looked over his shoulder. "What's up, Lucas?"

"I'm getting all this foam. Is it the tap?"

"Hm. Let me see." Scott shelved the bottles he'd been carrying and went to have a look. "Oh. Is that glass frozen?"

Lucas nodded. "Yeah. It's a Pilsner so...right?"

"Yeah, that's right. Try rinsing the glass first, then pour."

"Rinse it right out of the freezer?"

"Yep. The frost makes it foam. Do a quick rinse, dry it out, try again." That was a trick he'd learned years ago—he didn't even think about it anymore. Of course Lucas wouldn't know that one.

"Got it." Lucas got back to work. They'd been training him during the slower shifts, and he'd been doing pretty well for a newbie, so Ezra had decided to try him out on a Friday night. Talk about a trial by fire. It was about to get crazy in here. Lucas had a good work ethic and everyone liked him, so it was time to see how he managed under pressure.

"I think that does it for the liquor." Ezra was helping Scott stock for happy hour, and they were just about done. Happy hour had been very happy lately; he was counting on a good night. "Is someone working on the garnish tray?"

"Oh. Yes, in the kitchen. It's all done."

"Okay. I got that, and then I think we're good. Are you working tonight?"

He shrugged. "Well, I'm here tonight, so if you need me, I'm working."

"Right on. I think we'll be okay. Lucas has been pretty on it. If I need you, I'll yell."

"Sounds good. I'm going to check on Jar and see if he needs anything. You good?"

"Yeah. All good. Thanks for the help with getting stocked."

"That's what I'm here for."

That, and anything else that needed doing. Technically he worked at the bar, and he drew a paycheck, but like Jar, he was part owner now, and he basically picked up the slack. Dead ice machine? He was on it. Need more tequila? He'd fetch it. Big spill on the dance floor? Show him the mop. It was cool, he didn't mind it. He'd waited tables and bartended and grilled up burgers in the kitchen too. He liked being busy.

He wandered to the back to see what else might need doing. He found Jarlath sitting at his desk, typing with the little banker's lamp on, one of the treasures from his dad's office that they were able to throw into the truck before the storm.

His handsome husband. Jar had finally made the office his—there was a new stereo, a mini fridge, some new pictures on the walls. A busted-up barstool leaned in one corner, all three pieces sitting there to remind Jar that things would always get better. That was what Jar said. Jar was less forthcoming with the details about how the stool had ended up in that state in the first place, but that was okay. It didn't matter, did it? This was Jar's place.

"Hey."

Jar looked up from his laptop. "Oh, hey you."

"Can I come in?"

"As if I would say no to the handsomest man on earth." Jar got up and pulled him into the room. "All ready out there?"

"Yeah. And Ezra is feeling pretty confident about Lucas."

"One step closer to taking some time off."

"We'll get there."

"Mhm." Jar moved in close, circling warm arms around his waist. "We will. We've figured everything else out."

He bent and kissed Jar, their lips sliding gently, and they leaned into each other. Jar had been so relaxed lately, he was almost like—

The crash in the kitchen was loud enough to startle them both.

"Uh...Boss?"

Jar stepped back. "Well, shit."

"I'm on it." He grinned at Jar. "More of this later."

"Later." Jar winked at him. "It must be Friday."

"Must be. No worries, we got this."

"We do."

Man, this pub. If it wasn't one thing it was another. It had been like that since Scott came home from San Francisco.

And he wouldn't have it any other way.

THE END

Mergers & Acquisitions
By Jodi Payne

New York attorney Teague Whitaker is so close to making equity partnership he can taste it. He's spent two years cultivating a relationship with the Avenstone Group and he's finally landed them, bringing in a big-money deal in a big-money industry.

Jason Kovacs is...from Jersey. He's been a barista, a bike messenger, a third-shift stocker at D'Agostino. He tries out new jobs and quits them all the time, not because he hates them, but because he doesn't love them. But that changes when he lands a job dancing at The Wiggle Room.

When Teague bellies up to the bar, Jason can tell he's had a bad, bad day. Jason also knows money when he sees it, so he swoops in on the polished hottie, hoping to make bank. Stunned by the unexpected loss of his career-making deal, Teague is there to drink. He's looking for a distraction, and chatting up the buff and pretty boy that just swiped the cherry from his whiskey sour is a damn good start.

Neither expects sparks to fly with one unplanned kiss, but that's just the beginning of the unexpected for Teague and Jason. They're from the same city, but they're living in two different worlds. Their relationship may be unconventional, but if they can meet in the middle—halfway between Wall Street and Jersey—they just might make it work.

Find out more here!

A NOTE FROM THE AUTHOR

Hey there!

I just wanted to take a minute to say thank you for taking the time to read Not Over You. I hope you enjoyed it. I know everyone is busy and our TBR (to be read) lists are out of control, so it means a lot to me that I ended up at the top of your pile this time.

If you have a moment, please consider dropping by the site where you purchased this book and leaving a review. All honest reviews are much appreciated.

If you're looking for more of my work, why not join my newsletter? Just go here: http://bit.ly/whatsupjodi.

ABOUT JODI

JODI takes herself way too seriously and has been known to randomly break out in song. Her men are imperfect but genuine, stubborn but likable, often kinky, and frequently their own worst enemies. They are characters you can't help but fall in love with while they stumble along the path to their happily ever after. For those looking to get on her good side, Jodi's addictions include nonfat lattes, Malbec and tequila any way you pour it.

Website: jodipayne.net
Newsletter: http://bit.ly/whatsupjodi
All Jodi's Social Links: linktr.ee/jodipayne

I nterested in learning more about Jodi's gentlemen? Want free fiction and news? Join my newsletter!

What's Up with Jodi
http://bit.ly/whatsupjodi

MORE BOOKS BY JODI

<u>M/M Romance</u>
Stable Hill
Soft Limits: A Deviations Novel
Creative Process
Linchpin
Whence He Came
Mergers & Acquisitions

Sons of Cape Cod Series
Not Over You

<u>With BA Tortuga</u>
Les's Bar Series
Just Dex

The Triskelion Series
Breaking the Rules

East Meets Westerns
(single titles)
<u>Heart of a Redneck</u>
<u>Wrecked</u>
<u>Land of Enchantment</u>
<u>Window Dressing</u>
Flying Blind
Special Delivery, A Wrecked Holiday Novel
Keeping Promises

The Cowboy and the Dom Trilogy
First Rodeo, Book One
Razor's Edge, Book Two
No Ghosts, Book Three
The Soldier and the Angel, a Cowboy and Dom Novel

The Collaborations Series
Refraction
Syncopation

With Chris Owen
The Deviations Series
Submission
Domination
Discipline
Bondage
Safe Words

F/F Romance
Best Lesbian Love Stories, Summer Flings
Sapphic Planet

www.ingramcontent.com/pod-product-compliance
Lightning Source LLC
Chambersburg PA
CBHW031953240626
47153CB00003B/968